THE WOLF BELL

Ere's two moons hung thin as knives low on the horizon. And Tayba—with the help of the old woman, Gredillon—began to give birth. With the pains so red hot she thought she would die of them, she heard Gredillon's words over and over, *If I must choose between you, I will save the boy.* Tayba hated the baby for this and for the pain he caused her . . . she fought to be free of him.

As the morning came with a pale whisper of light across the window, so came the babe. At once Gredillon laid the wolf bell beside him; at once the baby clutched at it.

"He is a Seer born," Gredillon said triumphantly.

"A Seer born and marked," Tayba replied. "It can't be . . ."

"You do not know what you have borne here! This child—*this child* and the mystery he seeks will reshape the history of Ere!"

THE WOLF BELL

SHIRLEY ROUSSEAU
MURPHY

AVON
PUBLISHERS OF BARD, CAMELOT AND DISCUS BOOKS

The Atheneum edition carries the following Library of
Congress Cataloging in Publication Data:

SUMMARY: With the help of the wolves and the slave Jerthon,
Ramad must search out the Runestone
for the future good of the entire planet of Ere.
[I. Science fiction]   I. Title

AVON BOOKS
A division of
The Hearst Corporation
959 Eighth Avenue
New York, New York 10019

Copyright © 1979 by Shirley Rousseau Murphy
Published by arrangement with Atheneum Publishers
Library of Congress Catalog Card Number: 78-10415
ISBN: 0-380-50666-1

First Avon Printing, July, 1980

AVON TRADEMARK REG. U.S. PAT. OFF. AND IN
OTHER COUNTRIES, MARCA REGISTRADA, HECHO EN
U.S.A.

Printed in the U.S.A.

Contents

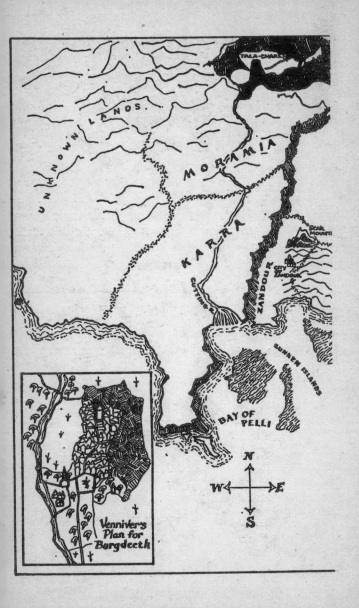

TALA-CHARE

UNKNOWN LANDS

MORAMIA

KARRA

SCAR MOUNTH

CUTTING R.

ZANDOUR

CITY ZANDOUR

SUNKEN ISLANDS

BAY OF PELLI

N
W — E
S

Venniver's
Plan for
Burgdeeth

MAP of ERE

THE WOLF BELL

Prologue

At a crossing in time when good and evil balance
On the burned land where they balance
A nation will be wrought.

Freedom and slavery crosswise on a tilted sword.
The bell will mark the Seer
Whose lifted hand decides it.

And the bell's shadow cast over all
With the wolves looking
From the mountain.

Conceived in vengeance to buy a life,
The Seer will come into the mountain.
But the woman will turn at the crossroads

And the bell's shadow cast over all
With the wolves looking
From the mountain:

She will be the vessel,
The bell's shadow cast tall across her,
The lives of men betrayed.

Part One

The Bell

Chapter One

IN THE EARLY DAYS of Ere wolves came down from the high deserts to raid the Zandourian sheep, slaughtering them or driving the animals up a sheer cliff to climb in terror or fall to their deaths. The Zandourian herders thought the wolves devils from the fires of Urdd itself and, helpless in their fear, turned to the Seers of Zandour. So the Seer NiMarn fashioned a bell of bronze held by a rearing bitch-wolf; with it, a man gifted in Seeing could call the wolves as a mother calls her babe, and they would come grovelling. After that wolves left the herds untouched and became slaves to the Seers of Zandour.

But with the bell and its dark powers, NiMarn ruled more than wolves. He ruled the cities of Zandour as well. The wolf cult held reign for five generations, until the volcanoes spewed fire and devastation across the lands of Ere. In the panic of sweeping rivers of fire, smoke-darkened skies and starvation, the wolf cult could not hold men. The cult crumbled, the wolves returned to the wind, and the bell was lost.

As the last leader of the wolf cult lay dying deep in the cave that would be his grave, he whispered a prediction that lived in that cave long after his bones had crumbled:

"A bastard child will be born, and he will rule the wolves as no Seer before him has done." His words were rasping and hate-filled, his sunken eyes cold with seeing his own betrayal. "A bastard child fathered by a Pellian bearing the last blood of the wolf cult. My blood! My blood seeping down generations hence from some bastard *I* sired and do not even know exists!

"A child born of a girl with the blood of Seers in her

13

veins. A child that will go among the great wolves of the high mountains, where the lakes are made of fire. Wolves," he whispered, shivering, "that are more than wolves. And that boy will seek a power greater even than the wolf bell, a power that even I could not master." Bile came into the Seer's mouth. He died with a look of cold fury on his thin face, and his bones rotted there in the cave of the wolf cult and he was forgotten for seven generations.

The volcanoes came once again. The lands were swept by fire. Men died and women became barren, and the few children born, it was said, were touched with evil. As the fires subsided, a girl-child was born in Zandour. She who would be mother to the bastard.

In those days a maid was chattel like the beasts, purchased at puberty for wifely work and breeding. When Tayba was thirteen her father took bids for her. She was tall and dark with teasing eyes and a beauty men watched with fine lust and bid high for. The bidders were wealthy young men whose fathers' herds blanketed the hills of Zandour and whose mounts and jewels were envied. Seven bidders, then twelve, each going higher until Elgend chose the most generous, chose jewels and gold worth a kingdom. So young Blerdlo was given the promise of Tayba; and if he was gross and fat-gutted and smelled bad, that was not considered, was of no consequence in these dealings. Elgend had done well enough with his other daughters; now Tayba would double his fortunes. And if she bore a healthy child, Blerdlo promised a bonus of such splendor that Elgend found the customary long wait for the wedding celebration nearly as difficult as did Blerdlo.

Tayba allowed her father's wives to give her the final training for marriage. She was silent and yielding to the prenuptial rituals and the Worshippings. She knelt docilely before the gods—and burned inside at gods who would allow her sale to that pig, Blerdlo, seethed hot with fury at the promising and vowed she would never honor it. Alone in her chambers, standing before her silver mirror, she mourned the betrayal of her own cool beauty, mourned the handsome young men who had wanted, and

14

lost, her. Well she would not be wasted on Blerdlo; she might prepare for her wedding bed, but she would not lie in it with him.

There was a fair young man in Zandour then, an unlanded drifter from Pelli lounging in the ale houses and gaming places. The servants said he was clever at bones and brittles and that he must be wealthy indeed, the way he used silver to satisfy his wants. Tayba managed many a trip to the marketplace, to the herb woman and the prayer fountain in preparation for her marriage. The young man began to watch her. He was sun-browned with pale gold hair, his eyes so compelling she found it hard to look away. When first he spoke to her, she looked down, letting her lashes brush her cheeks. She could feel his interest like a tide. She turned away, smiling a little. Soon they were meeting in the public places, then later in places where prying eyes would not follow. In Tayba's father's farthest sheepfold shelter, in the ogre's wood where few from Zandour ventured. Then at last in the blackened caves of Scar Mountain that rose between Zandour and Aybil.

He made love to her greedily. But when she tried to ease him into promises, EnDwyl did not commit himself. He let her imagine what she might. He watched her passion for him grow and was satisfied.

Soon Tayba was with child. The illness of it made her pale and so queasy she could not sit at table, but the wives put it down to nerves. She stayed to herself in her room until the early sickness was past. Her tall, lithe frame carried the secret well. After the first weeks of sickness she felt strong again and continued to slip away to EnDwyl. The gowns she chose were flowing, they showed nothing.

She was growing heavy the evening she put on a smooth, revealing gown at last and stood before her father's table to stare at him in cold defiance, the evidence of her betrayal mocking him. All up and down the length of the room there was silence, then a faint gasp from the wives who would be blamed for this: five days before the wedding and Tayba pregnant as a prize ewe.

Her father stared at her, the blood draining from his

15

face. He rose, white as loess dust, and stepped toward her. "Is it Blerdlo's?"

She gave him a cold smile and shook her head. His hand went to his skinning knife, and someone muffled a cry. She did not back away.

"You cursed . . . you worthless. . . . You've squandered a fortune with your willful ways! You'd have been bred soon enough to Blerdlo, but *you* couldn't wait. You—"

Her eyes flashed. "You sold me to that pig, to the ugliest, the smelliest among them! Well he'll never have me, and I'm as worthless to you now as a rotting sheep's carcass. You could get a better price from a servant's whelp!" Her smile was ruthless with the success of her revenge.

"Get out! Go with your unlanded lover and see how well *he* keeps you! You're no longer welcome in this house!" He slammed out of the room, and she looked after him with triumph, stared slowly around the table then, keeping her face hard, and went away with the cold looks of the household at her back.

She snatched up a few clothes, took a handful of silver from her father's stores before he thought to lock them, and ran barefoot through the night to the house where EnDwyl hired a sleeping room. She was drunk with her own freedom, giddy with her revenge. They would go to Pelli now, they would. . . . But EnDwyl was gone, his room quite empty of anything that had ever belonged to him.

She stood staring at the bare room, sick with shock. All his clothes, his boots, everything. When she went to rouse the innsman to find out where, he stood in his doorway swearing. "*I* know he's gone! And taken his horse and two roast ducks and a cask of ale as well and left nothing for the rent he owes!" He eyed Tayba speculatively, seeing her silk gown, the fur lining of her cloak.

She turned and left in haste, losing herself in shadow. The man wouldn't get EnDwyl's rent out of *her*.

She stood for a long while in the night-shuttered marketplace, near the fountain, swept by rage—and by a sudden cold fear. Her time was not far off. She had no desire

16

to drop the babe on the open hills like a dumb ewe. She had counted on EnDwyl to take her to Pelli to bear his child. He had said he would. Well, at least he had said—what had he said? In the heat of temper she could not exactly remember. Tears of self-pity came, she did not try to quench them, stood tasting the salt on her lips in terrible rage, then bent, shaken with a hard bout of sobs that seemed to ease the anger.

When she looked up from crying at last, she saw an old woman standing in the starlit square near the fountain, watching her. A short, dumpy figure, a woman such as was seen rummaging in the gutters of Zandour. The woman's voice was hollow as the night. She said cruelly, "EnDwyl has ridden toward Pelli, wanting to be free of you."

Tayba looked her over. "How would you know such a thing?"

"It is my business to know. And I have a message for you. You must go to the bell woman on Scar Mountain. She will help you. She says to bring honey and sow's milk. You take the fourth path at the turning by the water cave and keep on until the sun has set."

"The sun has not even risen," Tayba said irritably. "And why should I go to Scar Mountain?"

"To bear your child in safety. He was conceived on Scar Mountain, and on Scar Mountain he will be born." The old woman turned away, then cast back softly, "It will be light soon. You'd better hurry. And don't forget the sow's milk and honey." She was lost at once in the city's depths. Tayba stared after her outraged. She wished she'd been born a man; she looked down at her swollen belly and wished she were lithe enough to ride hard and strong enough to kill EnDwyl. She wished for the first, but not the last, time that this creature she carried was gone, even wished the baby dead and herself free of the whole matter.

The morning dawned foggy and cold. Shivering, she pulled her cloak around her and stared up at the craggy mountain. She did not know where else to go or what to do. She left town at last, angry at everything, at EnDwyl, the old woman, the gods—and very hungry. She purchased sow's milk and honey from a hillside farm wondering why she bothered, and some dry mawzee cakes to eat as she made her way up the rough path that cleaved around Scar Mountain.

The way up the mountain had been exciting when she rode behind EnDwyl. Now it was hostile and rough and seemed a good deal longer. When at last the morning mist blew away, the day became hot, the air heavy, and the path very steep indeed. She hadn't remembered how steep. She put on sandals, but the thin soles were little help against the sharp rocks. Her bundles grew heavier, and the sow's milk began to smell. She thought of her last ride here with EnDwyl, and she hoped a warring Herebian tribe would chop him into buzzard bait.

But when she passed the cave where they had lain, she mourned EnDwyl's golden hair and knowing ways. Why had the gods let this happen? Why had they let him leave her? She stared up at the sky. If she had seen gods then, flying on the wind, she would have cursed them roundly.

How had that old woman in the square known about her and EnDwyl? And how had this bell woman known? She had never even heard of a bell woman—*bells*? What did she do with bells? And what made her think the baby would be a boy? I don't *want* a boy! *I don't want any baby! What am I to do with a baby!*

When the sun had set she stood before a house made of stone slabs set against the side of the mountain. The afternoon had grown chill. She could see firelight through the cracks around the shuttered window. The door stood ajar. Tayba entered.

The stone ceiling rose high. The house was large inside, carven deep into the mountain itself; and the pale stone walls were sculptured into shelves on which stood bells, hundreds and hundred of bells catching the firelight, bells of amethyst and brass and painted clay, of jasper and of precious glass stained in deep tones. A thin white-haired woman sat folded onto a stool before the hearth. She watched Tayba silently. It was impossible to tell her age. Her eyes were too wise, too full of knowledge. She didn't need to speak to make Tayba feel so uncomfortable she turned away to stare with confusion around the stone room. Why had she come here? Why in Urdd had she come?

The evening light fell softly through the window to catch at the bells. Did they carry enchantments? There was nowhere else to look except at bells, or at the white-haired woman. Then she saw a bronze bell standing alone on the mantle, and a chill touched her. It was an ugly thing: a rearing bitch-wolf holding a bell in its mouth. She did not know why it terrified her, but she looked away from it, shuddering. She thought of the child she carried and stared at the woman sitting motionless against the stone mantle. Something dark in Tayba stirred then, some hint of things unspoken, things she did not want to touch or acknowledge, and she pushed them away from her mind in angry haste. The woman spoke.

"I am Gredillon." Her voice was clear, precise. "I am called bell woman." Her white hair seemed not to denote age so much as some strange condition of being. She looked long at Tayba, a detached, appraising look that did nothing at all to ease Tayba's awe of her. Did the woman always have that piercing, unnerving gaze? "You will bear your child here."

Tayba continued to stare.

"I will teach him what he needs to learn. I will teach you both, likely, for *you* are in desperate need of learning."

Tayba scowled.

"And one day he will lead you, this child you carry. One day he will lead men."

"No child will lead me! I do not even want this child!"

"Nonetheless, he will be born. And he will lead you into the Ring of Fire, and there you will find what *you* are made of. It is something you need badly to learn."

"No one goes into the Ring of Fire. And how do you know what *I* need?"

"You will go there," Gredillon said, ignoring Tayba's question. "Your brother Theel went, as far as the foot of it. Is it not true he followed the raider Venniver to the foot of those mountains to build a new city?"

19

"I suppose so. It's what he said. Who knows where Theel is."

"If he followed the dark leader Venniver, he did as he said he would do."

"If he followed Venniver to that place, he's probably dead." She laid her pack on the table. "Why did you bring me here?" Then, remembering the sow's milk and honey that she had set down absently, "And why did you want *those?* Do you expect me to drink sow's milk, old woman?"

Gredillon's smile was unexpected. It softened her angled face. "The sow's milk makes good cheese. The honey is to sweeten my tea." Her mouth twitched with amusement, but her dark eyes flashed. "Honey will not be wasted on *you,* young woman! It would turn bitter as dolba root in your mouth!"

"Why did you bring me here?"

"I did not bring you. I offered you sanctuary. Without me you would have had to return to your father's house and beg a herder's shack in which to bear your child."

"You bid me here," Tayba argued. "You told that gutter woman—what do you want of me?"

"I want nothing of you. I want only the safety of the child you carry. I want the safe birthing of your son." Gredillon rose and turned to the mantle so the bronze bell was cloaked in her shadow. When she turned back to face Tayba, her eyes were so fierce Tayba could hardly look. "I want him born safely, and you know nothing of birthing a child. You could die birthing this child and he could die with you. You are too young, they breed them too young. That is why the young women die, it is not from the will of the gods." She clasped her hands lightly. "This child must be born in safety, and you must live to care for him. But mark you this. If I must choose between you, one life to save, I will save the boy." She motioned to a low couch on the other side of the hearth. "You are too weary to contain such anger. Lie down now and sleep."

Tayba felt the weariness then, like a tide. She did as she was bidden, though against her will, turned her face to the wall away from Gredillon and, against her will,

20

slept at once. And in sleep the wolf bell burned darkly through the weft of her dreams, the bitch-wolf rearing tall, her mouth open in a toothy leer.

SHE BIRTHED THE CHILD with Gredillon's help as Ere's two moons hung thin as knives low on the horizon, birthed painfully through the length of the night with the pains so white hot she thought she would die of them. She heard Gredillon's words over and over, *If I must choose between you, I will save the boy.* Tayba hated the baby for this and for the pain he caused her, wanted only to be free of him, fought to be free of him. When she screamed with the pain, Gredillon stuffed a rag in her mouth to bite on.

Gredillon's thin, long hands held an earthen cup to Tayba's lips with potions, straightened her covers, or removed them when Tayba burned with the heat of her effort. The thin, patient woman was there as the pain came and went; the candlelight caught at her white hair and at the bells, and in delirium Tayba thought the bells were huge and saw Gredillon's white hair flowing through them and Gredillon's long hands reaching, reaching. . . .

At last, as morning came with a pale whisper of light across the little window, so came the babe slipping out onto the white goat blanket Gredillon held for him and crying lustily in the bright room. At once Gredillon laid the wolf bell beside him; and at once the baby clutched at it.

Tayba fed him, exhausted and half-gone in sleep, and did not look at the boy well until she woke at midday. Then she saw with shock that he was marked, the mark of the Seer, for he had hair like flame. Hair red as sable-vine. Burning red against the white goat blanket.

Gredillon ignored Tayba's dismay. "He is a Seer born," she said triumphantly.

"A Seer born, and marked," Tayba replied. "It can't be my blood. I have no blood of Seers."

"Do you not?" Gredillon looked hard at her, and again Tayba felt discomfort, some knowledge forcing itself into her mind that she did not want there. Angrily she put it away from her.

21

"And why must he have *red* hair? Not all Seers are so marked!"

"I grant you, he will be easily known for what he is unless he is disguised. All Seers are not so marked, but all with red hair are surely Seers. Well, we must take care of that when the time comes." Gredillon raised her face to the slanting light of the westerly sun that flooded the room, then touched the wolf bell that stood now beside the baby's sapling crib. "What is that sullen look, young woman? You do not know, or even care, what you have borne here. This child—*this child* and the mystery he seeks may well reshape the history of Ere!" And without consulting Tayba, "You will name him Ramad. Ramad means 'Of the Mountain,' and surely this child is of the mountain. He is a love child—a spite child—conceived and born on Scar Mountain."

Tayba held the baby close to her. Ramad? Ram? It seemed a strange name. She stared at Gredillon. "Who are you? How can you take the liberty even of naming him? What—what do you intend for him? Why should you . . . ?" And suddenly she felt the agony the babe would one day know, born a Seer—born to rule or to be killed by Seers. And she held him and nursed him tenderly then and loved his small, helpless body that curved so easily to her own. But she stared past him to Gredillon. "Who are you?" she repeated.

"Who am I? I come out of Pelli," Gredillon said, "where the Seers rule so strongly. From this mountain I have watched the Seers of Zandour grow stronger, after generations of weakness. Soon again they will be as strong as the Pellian Seers. As cold and unbending. One day soon Seers may rule all the coastal countries." She rose to slice cold meat for Tayba, and new bread, and watched the girl eat as if she had not seen food in days. "There is little love between the Zandourian Seers and the Pellian, but their ways are too much alike for comfort. The simple days on Ere are past, young woman. The days when there were no nations, but only roving tribes with the land between falling to one group then another, then belonging to no one as the volcanoes swept down.

"Even the days when Zandour ruled all the coast clear

to Sangur was a simple time compared to what lies ahead. Though those rulers were strong indeed, with the cult they brought upon Ere." She looked down at Ram. The baby was staring at her intently, as if the sound of her voice stirred him.

"Well, the volcanoes helped end that rule. But now the Seers grow stronger again and begin to band together. All but the Seer of Pelli. He does not band with anyone. He is close in spirit to the old Zandourian rulers—he would take the coast if he could, as Zandour once did. And those Seers who are of goodness will continue to be driven out or killed." She took the babe from Tayba then. "But this child—mind my words, young woman. This baby will one day help to bring together those Seers who cling to the good. He will, if no evil defeats him, bring a force of great wonder back into Ere, a force that will aid all men of goodness." She stared at Tayba coldly. "Who am I? I am no one. I am one who cares." Then she said, as if reluctant to speak of it, "I am of Herebian blood and also of the blood of Seers; the blood of the wild, raiding Herebian tribes that would have raped and murdered everyone in Ere if they could have managed it— and the blood of the Cherban Seers, some of whom hold great good and some of whom lust after evil as surely as the Herebian ever did. Perhaps I feel, because of my mixed blood, a need to see a stop to the evils, a need to help against the darkness."

Tayba finished her meal in silence and accepted the baby from Gredillon. Too many thoughts crowded her mind. She settled Ram beside her for sleep. This tiny newborn thing—how could Gredillon speak of his changing all of Ere? That was ridiculous. The woman was quite mad. He was only a baby.

But Ram grew into a handsome, sturdy boy, healthy as a young animal, and when he was of an age to learn, Gredillon taught him his letters. Then she taught him the ancient runes of the gods that few men of Ere could decipher. She taught him the myths of Zandour and Aybil and of the coastal countries, and of Carriol and the high desert tribes. She bade Tayba sit at the lessons, though she was an unwilling, fidgeting student who gazed off toward Zandour and thought unruly thoughts. Ramad listened well and was embarrassed by his mother's inattention, and by the sense of her thoughts that he caught and did not understand.

In time, Gredillon taught young Ram the skills to roam out of his mind into the minds of others, the minds of men down in Zandour, simple men at first whose thoughts were easiest to enter. Ram didn't like that much. He found the minds of men cruel and unhappy. And the Seeing was never constant, often it would not come at all as was the nature of the art, so that Ram might spend days reaching out in vain. A small boy's patience, even a small Seer's patience, has its limits. But Gredillon's own patience never flagged. She nurtured Ram's Seer's skills and built on them. She made him know that his salvation, his very life, lay only in the talents he could master.

She taught him the herbs and the simple potions, too, and taught these to Tayba and made her pay attention. Tayba and her child learned to find and gather and dry the herbs of Scar Mountain, and to use them.

Then Gredillon taught them the sword. She drilled them in mock battles until both Tayba and Ram were near exhaustion; and this practice held Tayba's attention, pleased her. Then at last Gredillon began to teach Ram the use of the wolf bell, though there was little need to teach him. The boy was drawn to the bell, and quickly he became skilled with it. There were no wolves on Scar Mountain in those days, but soon enough Ram could call down the foxes and jackals. The foxes came slipping close to rub against his legs and eat from his hand, coy and appealing, with pink-tongued smiles that made Ram laugh. But the jackals were sly and ugly. Big, rangy animals, gaunt and slit-eyed, that hung their heads and looked up at Ram menacingly. They frightened Tayba. She went tense while Ram held them with the bell's power, and when he loosed them they fled and did not hang back to clown as the foxes would.

At these times Ram seemed not a child. Scarce six years of life he had, then seven, but always when he brought the wild animals down to him, the man Ram would one day be shone out, calm and sure. His small boy's face was filled, then, with light, with a strong intensity that spoke of power—and drew only unease from Tayba. Once when the jackals had fled, she stared after their slinking shadows and said crossly, "Why do you *want* to call them? They—they make me so uneasy."

"They are brother to the wolf, Mamen. One day I will call wolves." He turned away from her to stare out over the mountain, and she pretended she did not see the hurt in his face, see his disappointment in her.

He looked back at last. "One day," he said, unsmiling, "I think the wolves will save you."

"How could wolves save me?" But at his words she hastily pushed something away that rose far back in her mind, a picture of wolves leaping, a wild unbidden thought that she did not want, that could not *be*. There was nothing in her, nothing, that could call forth a vision; she had not the blood for that.

"I don't know how they will save you, Mamen. But it comes into my mind that one day they will. It is the same as the visions of the gods. I See, but I don't understand—yet. One day I will understand."

She looked at him, her hand shaking. "Does—does Gredillon know you have visions of gods?"

"She knows. I see the winged gods. . . ." His eyes were alight now, eager. "They only seem half-horse and half-man, they are nothing like either. They are so beautiful!" The exalted expression in Ram's dark eyes made her catch her breath. She sat down beside him on the boulder and touched his red curling hair and shivered. She wished —but what good did it do to wish? He was as he was. She could not change that.

"I see the gods in the old cities. In Opensa and Carriol and Owdneet," he said with wonder. "I see how the cities were, the mountains carved with bowers and caves. And, Mamen, men dwelled there with the gods. Seers like me, Seers. . . ." He stared up at the sky. She watched him and knew, bitterly, that he belonged to this more than to her. To this wildness, to the Seeing of gods. He stared past her, puzzling. "The gods dwell in one path of air, and the Seers in another. But they dwell together. I do not fully understand—yet. It is like the fish Marga in the sea and

25

the bird Otran in the air. They speak to each other, but each lives in its own world. Only—it is the same world." He frowned, trying to work it out, looked possessed by this. Why was it so important to him? She wished they had never come to Gredillon, never seen the wolf bell. That bell—and Gredillon's teachings—led him into worlds she could not touch, made him dream precarious dreams. He would be better off without it, might even be a normal boy and forget he was born a Seer.

He put his arm around her waist, leaned close against her, was so tender suddenly and sweet. She loved the little boy smell of him, his smooth bright hair—but wished it were dark instead of red. She held him close, loving him and wishing to change him.

He took her face in his small hands, was so close his dark eyes were the whole world. "I would not be better off," he said, reading her thoughts so easily. "I am eight years old, Mamen. If we had not come here, I would be. . . . Without Gredillon to show me, I would not know what is inside of me, or what to do about it." His whole being had grown fiercely intense. "I do not ask *you* to change, Mamen. I do not ask you to keep yourself from the trips you make at night down the mountain when you—when you are unhappy. When you think I am sleeping and cannot know."

Shame rose in her like a tide. She wanted to look away and could not, he held her with his knowing gaze. She saw in his eyes knowledge far beyond a child's knowledge. "I. . . ." She swallowed and turned away then, and could deny nothing. Could not deny that in the night when her own inner turmoil, when her terrible need became unbearable, she would slip away to follow the dark path down the mountain and go into the drinking halls and go with men into the night. Men who warmed her and made her whole again so she could return quietly, at last, to the mountain.

Gredillon never spoke to her of this. Her disapproving looks the next morning were always quite enough. And now here was Ram confronting her so bluntly she wanted to scream at him.

He hugged her again. "It's all right, Mamen, I . . ." but

he did not finish, stopped abruptly to stare past her, down the mountain. She rose to look, but saw only sky and the empty rock, and Zandour lying like a toy city below.

But Ram saw something, looked cold suddenly, and white.

"What is it? Ram . . . ?"

"A rider is coming. He is maybe two days away. A man—a man riding out of Pelli. A man . . ." He searched her face. "He is a man you know well. A man with yellow hair."

Her heart leaped. EnDwyl. EnDwyl was coming.

"He is—he is the man who is my sire."

EnDwyl was coming for her. Coming to take them away, to care for her. . . .

"No, Mamen. He does not come for you." He went to stand by some boulders where the land fell abruptly. "He comes to the mountain for me." He turned to face her. "To take me away to Pelli. He would take me by force to Pelli. The Seer of Pelli has sent him—the dark Seer." There was growing fear in his eyes. He stood silent for some moments as if listening, then said hesitantly, "They —they would make a ruler of me. Whether or not I want it. I will have no choice in the matter, if EnDwyl finds me."

"I wouldn't let him take you. I—"

"What could you do? He is stronger. You—you have no power against this man." His knuckles were white. "Don't you understand! The Seers of Pelli are *forced* to rule, are twisted. Their minds are all twisted. . . ." He stepped so close to the steep drop she gasped, reached to pull him back. He scowled, turning from her. "They need —there is something about me they want. Something besides just that I am a Seer." He looked puzzled, fearful. "I will not go. And you will not make me go. I will not be their slave so that you—so you can live in comfort, Mamen!"

She stared at him, turning sick at something in herself, at the sudden truth he had touched. "Get Gredillon," she said coldly. "Go and get her! She is in the field above the garden."

Gredillon made the plan, took Tayba's silver and went down the mountain into Zandour, to return the next morning leading a pack pony that bore a small, closed burial coffin on its back, the dirt still clinging.

They carried the coffin up beyond the garden. Gredillon pried up the lid and applied ironroot dye to the hair of the corpse until it shone bright red. Then she closed the coffin and buried it and made a wooden marker. Ram said, "We must hide the pony. The Seer of Pelli saw this place, the house and the garden, has made EnDwyl see it. EnDwyl knows we had no pony when he left Pelli. He will wonder why we do now."

"We will hide her," Gredillon said, "inside the mountain, just as you will be hidden." So they stored dry grasses deep in a cave that opened from inside the stone house, and when EnDwyl was halfway up Scar Mountain, Ram took the pony there, hid in darkness, and Saw in his mind the approach of the man who was his sire.

Tayba stood alone in the doorway watching EnDwyl come around the last turn of the path, his horse sweating from the climb. His cape was gray with the grime of travel, his boots wrinkled and misshapen from long wear. He reined in his mount. The dropping sun touched his pale hair, his ice blue eyes. He watched Tayba intently. His eyes on her upset her, she turned away and busied herself drawing water as she might for any traveler. When she handed the mug up, his look made her remember.

He did not speak, but drained the mug in one swallow. At last he said coldly, "You have a child of me." His abruptness shocked and hurt her. "He is a Seer born. I have come for him."

He was so sure of himself, sitting there on the fidgeting mount. "I *had* a child," she said quietly. "He is dead. Ram is dead." She saw his eyes, not believing her, and her temper rose. "And even if he were alive, he—*he would not be your property!* You deserted us both when I— when. . . ." She dissolved into tears, half with true emotion at her desertion and half with the artful deceit she had practiced, turned away from him weeping and stricken with emotions she could not really sort out.

"You lie! My child is not dead!" He dismounted in

one motion and took her by the shoulder. "Dead *how?* Not *my* son!"

"He is dead." Her voice faltered. "My baby—Ramad died on the mountain. He fell from the mountain."

"You're lying! The boy was not dead when I left Pelli, the Seer of Pelli saw him. My son was born a Seer. No Seer would fall from a mountain."

His anger was of such power she could hardly hide her fear. "It is a long ride from Pelli. It is many days ride since any Seer saw Ram alive. Yes EnDwyl, he would have been a Seer. But a Seer, too, can fall from the mountain."

EnDwyl hobbled his horse with such haste the animal snorted and reared. He flung past her into the stone house and began to tear it apart in his search, scattering and breaking the frail bells, throwing the bedding on the floor, ripping open cupboards. He found Ram's small clothes and cast these onto the table. "You keep the clothes of a *dead* boy?"

"It's all I have of him! It's all I have left of him!" She grabbed up Ram's tunic and trousers and clutched them to her.

"Where is his grave, woman? Where is Ramad's grave?"

It was then that Gredillon spoke from the doorway, the low sun behind her making her white hair a halo, hiding her face in shadow.

"Can't you see what you're doing to her! The girl hasn't eaten, has been beside herself with grief. I've done my best with her, and now you come along and undo it, now she will grieve herself to sickness again."

"The grave, old woman. Where is my son's grave?"

"It's there beyond the herb yard. Past those three outcroppings, by the zayn tree," Gredillon said angrily.

When EnDwyl had gone Tayba clutched Gredillon's shoulders. "Will he believe it? He could have heard in the town that you bought a coffin, a body—"

"He did not hear such."

"But the earth is raw where we buried it, new turned and—"

"The earth is covered with wet leaves, the same as the garden."

Tayba waited in terror for EnDwyl to return.

And in the dark cave, Ram clung to the pony, his fear of EnDwyl like a sickness as he felt the man's relentless, evil searching. Clearly, he saw EnDwyl take up a garden spade and unearth the little coffin and open it to examine the wrapped, moldering body. Ram clung to the pony where the animal stood quiet in the unfamiliar dark, and each was comforted by the other. The pony nibbled at his tunic, responding to the child's soft touch and quick whispers.

In those moments, standing frightened in the darkness, Ram knew his father deeply, and hated him. And he felt Tayba's fear of the man, and felt her desire for him in spite of fear. And that vision gave the child little comfort.

EnDwyl left the stone house uncertain in his mind that Ram was dead and unable to find proof that he lived. The cave was well-hidden, Ram and the mare silent in the darkness—though Ram had begun to think he would forget what light was like, would come forth blinded from being so long in darkness. The mare did not eat well of the grasses they had stored, and when Ram led her, blinking, out into the light of Gredillon's stone room, both were weary from the dark. "He is gone," Ram said, staring around like a small owl. "It was awful in there. I am hungry for a hot meal."

Gredillon made a meal for him of tammi tea and boiled roots and a fried rock hare from the snares she set. Then she put Tayba to preparing packs for a journey. At Tayba's fretful look, she said, "Young woman, there is no help for it. You and Ram must leave this place as quickly as you can. EnDwyl will reach Pelli soon enough, and there he will learn of our lie from the Seer who sent him. He will return at once, and very likely he will bring an apprentice Seer with him—to track Ram. This is not a game. This is Ram's life in the balance. Don't you realize what they want of him? They would make a slave of him, would have his soul and leave a thing twisted and cruel as themselves to rule with them—to rule after they are dead. Ram is the tool they need; Ram and the bell he commands. They want. . . ." Gredillon paused in folding the blankets and stared absently around the room. "They would rule wolves again. In the old killing ways, when men were torn apart by wolves for transgressions against the masters, and women were. . . ." she glanced at Ram and went silent. They exchanged a long look, then Ram began to eat again, slowly; very pale.

Gredillon put her hand on Tayba's shoulder. "Ram is not strong enough yet to battle the Pellian Seers. One day he will be. One day, if he works at mastering his skills, he will be stronger than HarThass and all his cold apprentices."

"No one is stronger than the Pellian Seers," Tayba said, taking up mountain meat to wrap.

Gredillon ignored her remark. "When Ram is finished eating, get that dye on his hair. Keep it away from his forehead or it will stain." She was talking to Tayba as if she were a child. "Put the dye in the pack, you will need it. When you reach the river Owdneet, there will be sweet-burrow thickets. You must pick enough to make more. Now give me that pack, young woman, and I will saddle the mare."

Gredillon balanced the weight of the packs so the pony would travel well. When Tayba and Ram came out, cloaked and ready, she stared at Ram, his hair as dark as Tayba's. His tanned skin seemed darker, his eyes . . . his eyes looked more like his mother's now, under the dark thatch. Huge, black as cinders. Before, they had caught golden lights from his tangle of red hair. A dark-haired stranger of a boy. She turned to Tayba, inspecting her critically. "Go to the pump, young woman, and scrub the dye from those hands again—use sand if you must. I'll wager my kitchen table is a mess."

Tayba returned at last with clean hands, red and sore from scrubbing. Gredillon said, "You must go quickly over Scar Mountain, quickly down onto the black plain, for you won't be safe until you are in the city where your brother Theel dwells. And if Theel cannot protect you, you must then go on, up into the Ring of Fire."

Tayba began to lose patience. What good would it do to go into the Ring of Fire?

"You must prepare yourselves to live on the mountain

31

if need be," Gredillon said, frowning at her. "Do not fool yourself into thinking that is not possible. It is quite possible. The caves of the old city are there. They may be blocked from easy entrance, and some surely are eaten away by fallen lava, but they are there and safe. And," Gredillon straightened the bridle, then turned to hold Tayba's gaze, "the wolves are there. The great wolves. Ram's power will be greatest among them." She tightened the girths, then moved to rub the mare's ears for a moment. "If Theel cannot protect you, the wolves of the mountain will."

Tayba stared back at her and knew that she was crazy. They could not live among wolves. She said nothing.

Gredillon placed the bell in Ram's outstretched hands, then pulled the boy to her. Then she turned away toward the cottage to hide tears, and Ram and Tayba started up along Scar Mountain. Ram kept his face turned from Tayba for a long time before he blew his nose and looked ahead.

Quickly they lost sight of the house and garden plot. The way ahead was wild and lonely, and above the first peaks otero birds wheeled and screamed against the wind-driven sky.

Chapter Two

THE PATH WAS ROUGH, blocked by jagged outcroppings, narrow and uncertain; they climbed northward up over the rim of Scar Mountain, and as night came the wind blew wild and cold as if icy hands pushed at their backs. Ram trudged on silently, leading the willing pony. Tayba shivered, chilled through, aching from the long climb. She missed Gredillon's warm hearth. Near dark they found a shallow cave for shelter and built a little fire from brush and twigs, to half cook the rock hare Gredillon had tied to the pack. This would be their last fire for some time. For on the following evening they stood well down the mountain's north slope staring out over the black plain, both afraid to build a fire that would be seen by someone —something—that might be watching unexpectedly from that desolate expanse. The wind bit through their clothes bitter cold, the blackened plain swept away alien and immense. Ram pushed on, saying little, but Tayba stared out at the gathering dusk over that empty plain and knew, suddenly and painfully, that they could not go there. They would die there. They must turn back in the morning, while still they could.

"We will go on," Ram said, looking at her coldly. "And we will go on tonight for a little while. It looks—it looks more sheltered there, farther down." He frowned and looked away, then forced the mare on, holding her head so she wouldn't stumble among the shadowed rocks. Mamen puzzled him. Why was she so reluctant? He could feel nothing but her hesitancy, her fear. Below them on the plain, dark boulders rose twisting into nightmare shapes, seemed to grow larger as the light faded.

Tayba followed him reluctantly, thinking they had too

33

little food to cross that immense expanse, thinking of a hundred excuses. What if the mare should break a leg? The plain was wrought with malevolence, she could sense it. Perhaps an evil had been laid upon it by the gods to protect the ruined city that lay ahead in the black mountains. Surely the gods would prevent them from crossing to that place.

Ram turned, scowling at her, then stopped abruptly, turned to stare behind them not toward Zandour, but in the direction of Pelli. Fear touched him, cold and hard. EnDwyl and an apprentice Seer had left Pelli this hour. "They are following us, Mamen. They ride big, rough horses that can cover many more miles than we can. The Seer knows my fear. He knows, Mamen, he makes in your mind the fear you feel. It is hard to—I cannot block him. He is too strong." He took the mare's bridle and pulled her on down the slope so fast she nearly fell, then turned to steady her. Behind him, Tayba stared back at the darkening mountain they had crossed and felt the vast emptiness and their utter aloneness here and tried to put down her fear and could not.

They kept on until it was too dark to see, then crouched behind a shallow outcropping, made a cold meal of mountain meat, and wrapped in their blankets. The mare grazed as best she could on the sparse grass. They slept little, and Ram tossed restlessly, feeling the Seer's cold presence, trying to strengthen his own forces against the man's power. They were awake at first light. Ram watched Tayba stare out toward the far mountains, nearly lost in low cloud, and felt her increased conviction that they could never reach those peaks.

"We can't go on, Ram. We will . . . we will die out there. Would it be so bad to be a Pellian Seer?"

He flung the saddle on the mare irritably and secured the packs. "We won't die. Come on. Walking will warm you. You'll feel better when we're moving." He watched her share out the meager meal, ate quickly, then set out. She followed him sullenly. They came down onto the plain at last between monster-shaped black boulders. The wind swept at them like knives of ice. They tried to walk in the shelter of the mare, and she in turn pressed against them and kept wanting to turn tail to the wind.

They had gone well out onto the plain among the twisted boulders when Tayba began suddenly to feel comforted and to know that it would be safe to turn back. Something so warm enfolded her, something so familiar and welcome. EnDwyl would care for them. EnDwyl meant only to help Ram, surely they should wait for him. Eagerly she looked ahead to Ram and saw him turn, stare back at her in anger. Well, she thought, he didn't understand. EnDwyl would make the Seers of Pelli help him. Ram could come into his full power only through those Seers, she realized. He would learn skills with them that Gredillon could never have taught him.

Ram stopped and turned, and his dark eyes were filled with cold fury. But he said nothing. When he turned away at last, he slapped the mare so hard she was forced into a wild trot. Tayba had to run to catch up. As she followed Ram, she began to weave dreams around EnDwyl. She remembered the caves of Scar Mountain and being in EnDwyl's arms. She stood again before the stone hut greeting EnDwyl, and this time he held her and caressed her.

Ram swung around. His white face was that of a stranger, his fury terrible. *"Stop it, Mamen! Go back if you like, if it's what you want! But you will go alone!"*

She stared at him, shocked. "Don't talk to me like that!"

"I'll talk to you any way I wish, when it's *my life* you would sell. EnDwyl does not care for you!"

"You don't understand, you're only a child! You don't understand anything!"

"Oh *don't* I understand! EnDwyl never loved you! EnDwyl made a fool of you!" His dark hair was jerked by the wind, his cloak pulled away from him. He spoke as an adult, wiser and harder than Tayba. "EnDwyl left you once. You were young and beautiful then. Why should he want you now! Can't you see. It's the Seer making you think like this. EnDwyl can't send thoughts. It's the Seer. Don't you know what they are doing to you—to me, Mamen. They would kill me."

"Oh surely not. They—"

His scowl silenced her, a terrible, dark scowl filled with fury—born of fear. She swallowed, tasted bitterness in her throat, said nothing more. She followed him, chastened and uncomfortable and wanting only to be left alone with her own feelings; to be warmed by En-Dwyl—to turn back to him.

When again EnDwyl's voice began to whisper, she thought of Ram's fear and tried to put his words away from her; but they warmed her until soon she was clutching at them eagerly, could think of nothing else. Ram plodded ahead of her hunched and miserable as En-Dwyl and the Seer drew closer.

Night after night, when they would rest for a few hours, Tayba would toss with dreams of EnDwyl and wake wanting him, her need for him a sickness. She no longer saw Ram's fear, she began to rejoice that the riders were drawing close, felt elation when the mare turned to stare back over her shoulder, sensing her own kind there behind them.

Ram spoke not at all. Or, when he did speak, anger shaped his words. "Don't you know I am fighting with all the strength I have? Use your mind, Mamen! Use something to resist him. Haven't you anything in you but—but the instincts of a creature in rut?"

"You daren't say that to me! You . . ." She lowered her eyes before him. "They want . . . they want only to help you," she breathed, hating Ram then.

"*Help me?* They would train me like an animal, that's what they want of me. An animal taught to rule as *they* rule, with a lust that thinks nothing of the feelings of men. They want my soul, Mamen."

She followed him without volition, simply because he was stronger.

For three days more Ram forced her on. He was pale, pinched with the effort he made against the Seer. He felt hard and unchildlike and wanted comforting. He longed for Tayba's tenderness and warmth, but she did not give it. Even when they lay close at night, each was drawn tight and did not comfort the other.

Sometimes in a brief moment of clarity, Tayba was appalled at her feelings and knew then that the Seer did, indeed, lay a sickness on her. Then her shame would wrap her in a cocoon of loneliness so she could not reach out to Ram. She was not sure how long it was since they had left Gredillon, or even why they had left.

They were always cold and could not rid themselves of the blowing sand that had worked itself into every fiber of their clothes and blankets, into the food. The mare grew weaker and slower with the meager grass she received and only scant water from the sluggish springs. They might have been on that plain forever among the black rock and emptiness. Ram held the wolf bell often, taking strength from it, from the vague voices like puffs of wind that came to him when he said the words of the bell. There ahead in the mountain something stirred and eased him, lifted his spirits and gave him hope.

Tayba watched him, uneasy when he touched the bell. She felt sick, felt old, wanted only to turn back. They came at last one late morning around boulders to where they could see a line of trees ahead instead of writhing stone. At once their pace quickened, the mare nickered. They drew closer and the mare thrust her nose out eagerly, and they could hear the churning of water. They had reached the river Owdneet.

They came through trees to the river and looked beyond it and beyond the trees and could see the roofs of Burgdeeth. The dark riders were close behind them; the mare's ears kept turning back as she measured the sounds of their approach. The river raced white and foaming over stones, but was shallow enough to ford. The mare sucked up water noisily. Ram sprawled to drink, and Tayba stared at the cold, fast rapids, then leaned against the pony until her dizziness passed, sick with exhaustion and with her own overwhelming emotions. She looked at Ram and was swept with remorse at her behavior.

Ram had even stopped shouting at her when she was drawn to EnDwyl, when she could not help the tide of heat and yearning that swept her. He had pushed on and on across the plain as if he and the mare were quite alone, as if Tayba no longer existed. Small and sturdy, plodding on in the bitter cold, his dark hair and his desperate determination making him seem a stranger.

She had thought once that she must dye his hair again, but then she had forgotten.

The mare lifted her dripping muzzle to gaze downriver. They heard a horse snort. Tayba grabbed at Ram, pulling him up. "Get on the mare. Get across the river, into the town." She shoved at him, forcing him.

But he pulled away, spun to face her. "No, Mamen. I will go no farther." He put his hand inside his tunic, drew out the wolf bell now; the cold sun caught at the bronze, so the bell flashed with light. He held it up and gazed past her toward the dark mountains. "The wolves will come. They speak to me."

"You can't call wolves! Jackals, a fox maybe. *That can't help us!* Not wolves, Ram. *They* won't . . ."

He whispered the words of the bell precisely and slowly and did not hear her. Downriver the brush rattled, and the mare shifted to look, pricking her ears with eagerness. Tayba tried to pull Ram away, heard a hoof strike rock.

"Get on the mare, Ram!"

He turned then and suddenly was quite ready to mount. "They will come," he said quietly. There was a look on his face she had never seen before. He was not a child now, but something ageless. He mounted the mare slowly. Brush rattled.

"Hurry!" She had nearly lost patience with him. The mare nickered as riders came crashing through brush. Then suddenly the noise stopped, the riders were still. Ram hit the mare hard, forcing her into the river. Tayba ran alongside splashing, clinging to the mare against the swift current as the freezing water surged around her legs. The riders came crashing through bushes again. Icy water foamed around her thighs and washed the mare's belly so she balked; Tayba jerked and jerked at her. At last she went on again and soon they were in shallower water. The mare scrambled wild-eyed up the bank as Tayba clung; and the riders plunged into the river. Tayba tried desperately to see the town ahead, but now it was hidden; she could see only the plain rising above the trees, cloud shadows blowing fast across the empty land. She saw Ram stare up at the rising land, heard him draw in his breath sharply. Those were more than cloud shadows. They *were* running shadows: dark animals racing down across the cloud-swept plain. Dark wolves running. . . .

Wolves, flicking from sun to shade, huge wolves sweeping down toward them, now, through the woods. The mare reared as they leaped toward her, spun away, pulling the rope in a sharp burn through Tayba's hands; Ram jumped from the saddle as the pony veered under him. "Let her go, Mamen! Let her go!" The terrified pony leaped wildly past the approaching riders and disappeared into the trees—and the wolves surged around Ram, their eyes like fire. Tayba stood backed against a boulder, could not speak for the terror that held her. Huge shaggy wolves pressed against her, tall as her waist, rank-smelling; and their yellow eyes looked at her with a knowing that shook her.

She saw Ram put out his hand to the dark wolf leader, saw the wolf come to him, saw Ram thrust his hands deep into the wolf's coat in greeting, then lay his face against the animal's broad head as its tongue lolled in a fierce smile—the smile of a killer; saw the riders trying to approach, fighting their panicky horses.

Ram plunged his face against the warmth of the great wolf, smelled his wild smell, and felt whole suddenly, as if a part of himself had returned. Then he lifted his head to face EnDwyl and the Seer, pulling the big wolf close as he did so.

He sensed their fear with pleasure, saw the Seer's hesitancy and how the dark wolf watched the riders with lips drawn back. Ram's own lips twitched into a smile. "Fawdref," he said, caressing the wolf's ears. "You are Fawdref." Fawdref turned his head to nudge Ram and to nose at the wolf bell. Ram held the bell, and together he and Fawdref made a power that lifted and amazed him, a power that held the Pellian Seer immobile, unable to touch them with his darkness, his thin face ashen, his pale eyes bulging with the effort—but then suddenly a new power surged within the Seer: Ram could feel

39

it like a tide, something sweeping out of Pelli to support the Seer—the man beat his terrified horse so it plunged toward Ram, his sword raised. Ram cried out, the wolves leaped; they were wild with killing now, wild for blood. Behind him Tayba stood frozen, her sword drawn. The Seer's horse went down with wolves tearing at it; the Seer screamed, and his scream seemed to echo beyond this place. Ram felt cold fear as EnDwyl flayed his horse through the pack, his face twisted with hate. As the animal reared over Tayba, EnDwyl shouted, *"You told me he was dead! You . . ."* Wolves leaped snarling to pull his horse down. He leaped clear, his sword flashing, slashed at wolves, forcing himself toward Tayba. She ducked his blade, her own blade blazing out. And the pack was on the horses and tearing at the flailing Seer. The smell of blood sickened Ram. EnDwyl swung around to loom over him then. Ram felt a sharp blow, went dizzy, saw Tayba's sword plunge into EnDwyl; he clung to consciousness, saw EnDwyl lash out—then saw EnDwyl poised over Tayba with the point of his sword at her throat.

The wolves, crouched to leap, held motionless, waiting for Ram to bid them.

EnDwyl looked coldly at Ram. "If I die, your mother will die." Blood oozed from his side. "If the wolves touch me, she dies." His pale hair was ribboned with sweat. He shivered. Ram tried to get up, reached to touch Fawdref's shaggy neck, was so dizzy that Fawdref blurred. He gripped the bell and spoke quietly, and the great wolf growled deep in his throat, did not take his eyes from EnDwyl.

"She will die, boy."

Ram saw the fear in Tayba's eyes. He saw her swallow, saw the blood soaking her tunic. He looked at the fear in EnDwyl that was different from Tayba's fear, at the evil in EnDwyl. He touched Fawdref's shoulder and felt the massive bone, felt Fawdref's impatience, felt the tenseness of the pack of wolves—then felt Fawdref's sharp dismay as he bid the animals draw back.

"Let her live," he said to EnDwyl, "but go quickly.

I can't hold them long. The Seer is dead and your horses are dead, and they want you now."

EnDwyl stared at Ram with hatred, his sword steady against Tayba's throat. "You may be my son, but I waste no love on you. If you send the wolves for me after she is freed, you will die. The Seer of Pelli knows you have killed his apprentice. If *I* die too, he will send an army to kill you. An army no wolf could stand against."

Ram smiled scoffingly. But he knew with dark certainty that what EnDwyl said was true. He crouched there, dizzy, and could feel a fury rise to him out of Pelli colder and more brutal than anything he had ever encountered. "Go in safety," he said, swallowing. There was a bitter taste in his throat. The ground spun, he saw blood. He must send the wolves away. He saw EnDwyl go, knew that he caught the exhausted pony up there in the woods. He bid the wolves away then, as the earth spun under him. . . .

When EnDwyl had gone, the dark wolf stood staring after him with cold eyes, then bent to lick Ram's face. Finally he turned and left Ram, his pack slipping up the plain beside him as silent as the cloud shadows they melted into, silent as the black boulders that shielded them from the town. Fawdref looked back once in a wordless promise that touched Ram even as Ram's mind swirled in blackness.

THE FOUR OLD WOMEN were walking slowly downriver filling reed baskets with dolba leaf and evrole and lemon-tongue. They talked incessantly; or, three of them did, gathering exceedingly slowly, gossiping about nothing until Dlos, who led them, thought she would go mad. You couldn't hear your own thoughts with those three prattling. She drew ahead, finding clumps of herbs the others might miss and marking them with rags tied to bushes. She was quite alone when she saw the two bodies, one bleeding, saw the gutted horses beside the boulder.

She saw the red roots of the little boy's hair in one quick glance and knew that if the child were alive now, he might not be alive for long with that hair. Quickly she turned back, distracting the three slow cronies, got them turned aside to a bed of cherba they had missed. "I will search for perrisax for soap," she said shortly. "Return here when your baskets are full. Be sure you pick all the cherba—but leave the roots! Don't pull up the roots!"

She watched the women amble away, then hurried up the path and knelt by the little child. He was so cold. There was an ugly bruise on his forehead, going purple, swollen and bloodied under the skin. She covered him with her shawl, pulled off her woolen underskirt, and dipped it into the cold river to make a compress. She chafed his hands, trying to bring the blood up, to stir him. He must be seven or eight. A sturdy child. The red hair showed plainly where the roots had grown out beneath the dye. She pulled the compress on his forehead up to cover his hair and bound it.

At last she turned to the girl, a dark, stirring beauty of a girl, the kind that would light men's souls—or goad them to hate and killing. Dlos examined the ugly wound in her side and washed and dressed it with dolba leaf hastily ground between stones. She dug into the pack on one of the dead horses, found clean cloth, and made a bandage.

The cloth in the pack was man's clothing, this was a man's pack. She examined the other pack, thick with blood and half-hidden under the dead, twisted animal and saw that it too had belonged to a man. No woman's clothes or child's things here. She found dye in that pack though, dye made from sweetburrow paste, a small stone crock of it. She glanced again at the child. There was no doubt the child was a Seer. Had this rider, then, tended the Seer child, kept his hair dyed, seen to him? And where was that rider? She removed the boy's bandage, opened the crock, applied the dye quickly until the roots no longer showed, then dropped the crock into her tunic pocket where it would not be seen. She wiped the dye from his forehead, being careful of the swelling bruise. Now his hair seemed as dark as the girl's. Was this young woman his sister? His mother? Where were the men whose packs and horses these were? Surely there had been two men. What had happened in this meadow? Dlos rose and began to search.

She found the man at once, lying mangled beside the horses, his body nearly hidden by torn hindquarters. She looked more closely and saw the red roots along his hairline. His tunic and the amulet he wore were those of an apprentice Seer of Pelli. There were coarse animal hairs caught in his belt. She found the tracks of the great wolves among the gore and glanced toward the path. The cursed women would be coming.

Quickly she stripped the Seer's tunic and amulet from his body and buried them in leaves, then applied the dye to his hair. That finished, she began to search downriver for the second man but found only the hoofprints of a third and smaller horse going away at a gallop, the marks very deep as if the animal carried a heavy weight.

She returned to the girl and child and the mangled body, to find the three women staring as uncertainly as she had expected. She put them to work stripping the dead horses of packs and saddles, of bridles. No sense leaving good leather for wolves to chew.

When she knelt to lift the child, she felt a hard lump beneath him. It was a bronze bell; she shielded it instinctively from the three women until she could look at it more closely. The rearing bitch-wolf made her stare and shiver. Suddenly and wildly the old fables from Pelli and Zandour filled her head, making her catch her breath.

What was this child, to carry such magic? Or had the older Seer carried it and the boy simply fallen where it lay? But, she thought puzzling, the wolves had attacked only the two men. They had not touched the girl or the child. That was a sword wound in the girl's side, not the jagged tear a wolf makes.

Surely the wolves had moved to the call of this bell. Why had a Seer of Pelli been traveling *here* with such a boy? And why did the Seer lie dead? She knelt there staring at the boy in her arms. What sort of child was this that she held so close to her? And what havoc would he create if she brought him to Burgdeeth?

Dlos touched the child's soft cheek, shadowed by dark

lashes, looked at the bloody, swollen bruise on his forehead. She raised her eyes and summoned the other women. She would need help.

RAM FELT HIMSELF CARRIED, saw bare branches swing close above his face; then suddenly he fell away from the light sky into darkness again and was dropping down and down. There were voices fading. Once lightness blazed, and he saw his mother's face close to him, rocking; the falling came again, tumbling him. He was so dizzy. He fell deep down beneath the earth into a cave so black. A man lay there. He lifted his head and whispered, and his face was thin and pale. The walls of the cave were painted with pictures of wolves leaping and snarling, bloodthirsty wolves that made Ram cry out in fear. He whispered, "Fawdref!" And didn't know what he said, or why. The man held up his hands, and they had turned to white bone. He shouted, "Bastard! A bastard born. . . ." And he was a skeleton, white bone lying in rags. His skull gleamed. The wolves on the cave walls waited.

Ram felt hands lift him, felt himself covered, relaxed into warmth. But something pulled and lifted him away from the hands, lifted his very soul and plunged it back into the blackness so he was torn away, his mind torn from his body.

He was in the cave again, and a man in silver sat high on a dais looking down at him and laughing. The painted wolves crouched, slavering. Ram pushed past them into the very stone with all his strength, searching for the real wolf's body, saw Fawdref leap snarling at the painted wolves as they came off the walls to slash and tear. Ram cried out, saw light come. The wolves all disappeared.

There was a plain stone wall beside him, low rafters overhead, the smell of mawzee grain. He could see the arch of a door. He came awake at last and clear in his mind and felt himself laid down and the cover drawn up over him. He stared up at a face, a wrinkled old woman.

Then the man in silver pulled at him insistently. Ram

cried out, felt hands soothe him, heard a voice trying to reach him. He saw a child's face close to him and wanted to touch her, then fell away and all was terror, the painted wolves leaping again and the man in silver striking out at him so he clung to Fawdref. He saw blood on the wolf and was dizzy, so dizzy. . . .

Chapter Three

TAYBA WOKE. She ached, every bone ached. She was in a dim room cluttered with objects she could only slowly make out. Kegs and tools, a loom. Cobwebs hung thick from the low rafters. The room smelled of dust and of grain. The one small window showed dull gray sky, whether of morning or evening she could not tell. Her mouth tasted stale. She tried to sit up and gasped at the pain, remembered EnDwyl's sword ripping her side, blood flowing; she touched her side carefully and felt bandages. Then she remembered EnDwyl standing over her, his sword at her throat, and Ram—*where was Ram?* EnDwyl had hit him, had. . . . Swept with panic, she pulled herself up so pain tore through her side and stared around the room. She could not see Ram, could see nothing but the jumble of kegs and tools.

Had EnDwyl taken Ram? Had EnDwyl escaped the wolves with Ram held captive? Her thoughts were dizzy and confused. She pulled herself out of the cot, leaned against the stone wall until the pain became bearable.

She was naked, her garment not in sight. She shivered in spite of the warmth of the room and pulled the blanket around her, staring dumbly at the clutter and at the iron stove in the far corner with its low blaze. Her cot was rough-split timbers, a root bin with straw hastily stuffed in to make a bed. Her blanket was thick and soft, though, and well-made. She recalled Ram again, shook her head to drive out the fuzziness, and began to search the room for him.

He was lying in a little boxlike bed wedged next to the mawzee thresher, a bed so like a child's coffin she gasped. She knelt beside him, her stomach heaving with

46

pain, and could feel oozing as if blood flowed from her wound. The swollen purple lump on his forehead made her feel sick. He was so pale, so very still. She lay her face against his chest and, finally, could feel the faint, welcome beating.

When she stood up she saw a square little woman poised in the doorway watching her. Tayba started to speak, then found she was unaccountably lying on the floor, the woman trying to lift her.

When she was back in bed at last, the woman held a mug for her. Tayba studied the leathery face bent over her, then drank. The taste was bitter, the liquid dark and hot. She thought she remembered that she had been given some before. By a child, perhaps? There was no one else in the room. Her pain began to subside almost at once. She felt sleepy, deliciously floating.

Morning sounds brought her awake again, the clank of buckets, a stove being stoked. Her head ached, her side was sore. She thought longingly of a tub of hot water. The little window was bright with sun now, and she could hear milk cows and the screams of chidrack fowl, the creak of wagons. A man's voice spoke beside the window, a shadow crossed it, then some steady pounding began and she could hear the harsh shouts of men giving orders.

She must have dozed, woke feeling dizzy as if she were falling, had to pull herself fully awake with a great effort, terrified suddenly of falling into sleep again. It was quite dark, though a few faint stars showed through the little window.

What had awakened her? She lay there confused and fearful, wondering if Ram had cried out for her. She slept and woke again and was being bathed, the square old woman leaning over her. The soap was perrisax, smelled spicy. She lay enjoying the warmth and luxury of the soapy cloth washing her body, felt the bandage removed, and opened her eyes to watch the woman binding fresh cloth around her, nudging her to move now and then. She did not want to look at the wound, the thought of it made her weak.

Later she woke in darkness not knowing where she was and the pain so bad she moaned, lurched against the stone wall so she scraped her arm and then swore. She saw a candle lit, was given a draught by someone small, little hands, a child's hands holding the mug and candle. She slept.

Then she woke at last to a morning when her senses were sharp and aware and lay watching the sun slant bright through the cobwebs that hung from the rafters. This room with its clutter of tools and furniture was entirely comforting.

The square, small woman was sitting by the window holding Ram in her lap, feeding him spoonful by spoonful as if he were a baby. Tayba rose, the ache in her side making her wince. She pulled the blanket around herself, supported herself against a barrel, then the thresher as she made her way across the room. The pain seemed to have been with her forever. She sat down on the bench close to the woman. What a wrinkled, leathery face she had; yet her mouth and eyes showed the lines of wry humor. The woman lifted Ram into Tayba's lap, and handed her the bowl so she could feed him. But she could only sit holding his chin and staring into his dull, expressionless eyes. Was he even aware of her? He looked like a stranger; and she had forgotten his hair was black. The swollen wound on his forehead sickened her unbearably; so tender a place to be injured. She cradled him close, nearly weeping in her distress for him.

"He is better than he was," the woman said. "It's been all I could do to get some food down him, some herb tea." Her hands were square and as wrinkled as her face. She wore shapeless coarsespun, a tunic over a long skirt, both dull brown in color and smelling of lanolin from the sheep.

"I am Dlos. I serve the master, Venniver, as we all do in Burgdeeth. My room is there, off this storeroom. We are behind the sculler of the Hall."

"How did Ram and I come here? I can only remember being by the river, lying there—how long have I been in this room, how long has Ram been so hurt and sick?" She stared with growing fear at Ram's closed, mindless expression. "Did anyone come with us? A man? Anyone . . . ?"

48

"I brought you here five days ago, me and three old women. There was a man with you." Dlos studied Tayba carefully, reading her fear. "A dead man."

"Was he . . ." Tayba's voice caught. "Dead? Oh—was he tall and fair? Pale hair? He—"

"He was old and swarthy. Thin-faced like a rat. A Seer. An apprentice Seer of Pelli lay dead there wearing his Seer's robes and amulet and torn to shreds by wolves. Their tracks were there—wolves that did not touch you two. I stripped him, disguised him, and buried his belongings. We do not need the trouble that a dead Seer would cause."

Tayba's head spun. "Disguised him?" She saw shadows on the plain and the great wolves leaping and tearing at the horses, at EnDwyl and the Seer, wolves pinning her against the boulder so she stood frozen in fear. She touched Ram's forehead with shaking fingers and raised her eyes to Dlos. "How could you disguise a Seer, his hair. . . ." Then her eyes widened, her fingers flew to Ram's hair, parted it, searching.

Ram's hair had wanted dying, she had meant to dye it. Now there was no red. She stared at Dlos, her lips parted in fear.

"The Seer carried a crock of dye. I used it on him to avoid questions about who he might be. And I used it on the boy, before the old women saw him."

"You dyed Ram's hair? But you—why would you disguise him?" she whispered. "We are nothing to you."

"I have my reasons for doing what I do." The old woman straightened the blanket around Ram's feet. "The other man, the fair one you spoke of—perhaps he rode back downriver. I found the tracks of a third and smaller horse, carrying a heavy load and trailing blood. Was that your horse, the small one?"

"Yes, our pack pony." She held Ram tight to her, trying to think. "EnDwyl will return. He will follow us," she breathed suddenly. "He will come—"

"The two men were pursuing you?" Dlos asked, puzzling. "And you and *this* child sought sanctuary here, where Seers are so hated? But didn't you know . . . ?"

"I meant to keep Ram's hair dyed. My brother—my

brother Theel is here." She looked at the older woman. "You know about us. You know what Ram is. Have you told the leader Venniver?"

"Why would I dye the boy's hair, if I meant to tell his secret?"

"But if—if Venniver finds out, what will he . . . what will he do to Ram?"

"If the boy is found out, he will be enslaved to work the stone." The old woman pushed back her untidy hair and glanced out the window. "Mark you, I will tell no one. I have my own reasons for keeping that promise. Now, just why were you running from a Pellian Seer and from this EnDwyl you speak of?"

"They wanted to—train Ram."

Dlos's hand came up from her lap as if of its own accord, to touch Ram's cheek. She said nothing. Then at last she raised her questioning eyes to Tayba. "So Theel is your brother. Does he know you have a child? A *Seeing* child? Does Theel know there is Seer's blood as his family's legacy?" She smiled crookedly. "He has never acted as if he knew such a thing."

"No one—there is no Seer's blood in my father's house," she said quickly. "That's not possible. We would have known, my sisters and I. A Seeing child. . . ." Why was her pulse pounding so? "A Seeing child would have brought a fortune. No! It's his father's blood. EnDwyl's. I have always known that.

"But my brother Theel—I have not seen him for eleven years; he can't know I have a child. How could he?"

"Yes. Perhaps. And do you and Theel have the same mother?"

"No, but—*there is no Seer's blood in our family. None!*"

"I didn't mean to anger you, young woman," Dlos said quietly. "So strange," she mused. "To have many wives in a household. I come from the Isles of Sangur where a man weds only one woman."

"What—what made you come here, to this place?" Tayba tried to calm herself, sat clutching Ram too tightly.

"I came with my husband. He followed Venniver and a wild dream into this land." The old woman paused to look out at the morning. "Then he died some years back."

Tayba looked hard at her, and impulsively put her hand over the square brown one. She could smell meat boiling from the doorway that must lead to the sculler and hear the voices of old women there. Suddenly Dlos shook herself as if she had come to some decision, and she looked over toward the far corner of the storeroom. Tayba followed her gaze and saw, crouched in the shadows, a thin little girl hardly visible among the clutter of tools.

"That is Skeelie." Dlos beckoned, and the child rose and came to her, pressing against her. "Skeelie goes quietly and becomes a part of the stone and the rubble, and that is the way we want it." She hugged the child close. "If Venniver forgets about her, forgets he sent her to me, then all is well with us."

Skeelie looked at Tayba without much expression, then turned her gaze on Ram. And at once her face softened, changed utterly. Tayba offered Ram, and Skeelie sat down beside her and took him in her lap. He was nearly as big as she, but she held him as if she were quite used to the shape of him in her arms.

"Skeelie has nursed him, too," Dlos said. Skeelie cuddled Ram close, and when she looked up at last, her eyes were full of such pleasure—and full, too, of a strange, unsettling knowledge. When she spoke, Tayba was shocked at the intensity of her reedy voice. "He sees something." Skeelie touched Ram's bruised forehead and wiped a smudge of gruel from his mouth. "He sees something that came here with you. He sees a darkness."

Some time later she whispered, as if she could not put it aside, "He sees an evil. There is an evil come here with you."

In the days that followed, the child Skeelie became as necessary to Tayba as Dlos was. The wiry little girl moved quickly and silently to care for Ram, who still had uttered no word since he woke, and to care for Tayba, bringing food, bringing hot water in jugs to fill a bathing tub, then lugging out the dirty water, finding clean cloth for Tayba's bandages and laving on the salve Dlos provided. Tayba's wound was painful and slow healing. And Ram remained in that somnolent state between

51

sleeping and waking that tore at Tayba. Sometimes she did not know whether he would live or die. She wanted to pull life from the world around her and force it into him. Only Skeelie seemed to understand the thing that possessed him. The child was sure and strong with him, seemed to know his needs despite the boy's silence. Tayba woke one morning to see her standing by the window with Ram seated on the sill and heard Ram speak for the first time. His voice was small and still, cold as winter.

"There is something here with us. Something—can't you feel it, Skeelie?"

"What kind of something?"

"Something dark that wants to speak inside me, to *be* inside me. I don't want it there! *I don't want it!*"

Tayba rose and came to stand beside them, to stare mutely at Ram. She wanted to hold him, but Ram did not reach for her. He clung to Skeelie. She turned away at last, feeling useless and afraid.

Gredillon had taught her nothing to deal with such as this. Was it only the blow on the head that made Ram like this? Or had the power of the bell turned on him? Had the wolves loosed some evil against him because he had called them? Some revenge that Ram did not understand and had no power against?

She had looked for the wolf bell among their washed and mended clothes. Their swords were there, the scabbards, a small knife Ram had always carried. The bell was not. The old woman had not found it.

Well she was glad, she didn't want it found. Unless— had EnDwyl taken the wolf bell while Ram lay unconscious? She could not remember, shook her head in confusion; could remember the blood and the great shaggy wolves all around her, but could not bring the rest of the scene clear in her mind.

And even if EnDwyl had the bell, he could command nothing of it. Or so Gredillon had believed.

She turned back to the window to stare uncertainly out at the mountains. Somewhere up among those peaks did the wolves wait, against their wills, for Ram to call them? They had terrified her. They had looked at Ram as if. . . . She shuddered. They might have saved Ram once, but surely they rebelled at being controlled by a human power. Wouldn't they yearn to destroy that power, to free themselves from it? Surely the jackals of Scar Mountain had rebelled as Ram held them. She stared hard at the mountain. *The bell is gone!* She thought angrily. *Ram can't use it against you! Leave him alone! If you have laid a curse on him, leave him alone! He can't touch you now!*

The rising sun caught the edges of the low eastern hills, then the mountain. She knelt, pressing her forehead against the windowsill. Maybe the gods would hear her prayer, even if the wolves didn't.

Then she rose and turned away from Skeelie, feeling embarrassed. But Skeelie put her hand out and drew her back to the window. "The slaves are coming," she said softly. "The women will stop here to work the gardens."

The line of slaves was marching single-file, flanked by guards. The five young women were all handsome in spite of the rags they wore. They went bare-legged in the bitter cold. A guard separated them from the men, handed out hoes, and they began to weed the gardens that lay in a row behind the Hall. The men were marched away. Skeelie hung out the window, watching. "The tall one, the one with the knotted hair," she said, "he is my brother Jerthon." Tayba saw the tall young man clearly for a moment before the line turned the corner at the upper end of the Hall. His long red hair was knotted at his neck, his profile like Skeelie's, clean and perfect. He walked too proudly, as if he did the guards a favor to obey them. There was a look of cold defiance about him, of anger—and of fine-drawn patience tautly held.

So Venniver kept Seers as slaves. There had been several red-headed men in the line, and one of the girls had red hair. A woman Seer, Tayba thought, amazed. And how many more were Seers, without the red hair to give it away? And how, she wondered, did her brother Theel feel about keeping slaves? Well, she supposed it was all right with Theel as long as they were Seers. He had always rankled at being ruled by the Zandourian

53

Seers, though they weren't nearly as strong, or as cruel, as the Seers of Pelli—simply sated in the luxuries the Zandourian people provided in ritual offerings.

When would Theel acknowledge that she was in Burgdeeth? When would he come to her or summon her? Dlos had told him, she knew. Everyone in town must know there were strangers here, carried in nearly dead. Would Theel welcome them? He was a stern, unloving man; he had grown up and left home while she was still a child. And what would the leader Venniver have to say? Well, she thought, that would be up to Theel, Theel was his lieutenant; surely he would speak for her.

It took some days for Theel to acknowledge her. She grew nervous and irritable, waiting, would look up tensely when anyone entered the storeroom, convinced herself at last that he did not want her there. She had decided to find out, to seek Theel out herself—she had not been out of the storeroom into the Hall or the town yet—when at last Dlos came to say that Theel had summoned her. She stood staring at Dlos, feeling suddenly terrified. Would Theel turn them out? All at once she was very afraid that he would—and afraid of Theel himself.

She followed Dlos through the sculler then along the back corridors of the Hall, catching her first glimpse of kitchen, then dining hall, where some old women were laying the tables amidst loud clanging of cutlery. The dining hall smelled of ale. There seemed to be none but old women in this place—except for the young slave girls. They turned right into the bedroom wing. Where doors stood ajar, she could see small bare rooms. Dlos left her at Theel's door as if she did not care to enter.

Theel's room was sparsely furnished. Bare stone floors, bare stone walls. A narrow bed, a rough chest. A sectbow hanging by the door. So chill she shivered.

Theel was even thinner than she remembered. A sour, unsmiling man, his face lined with bitterness where before it had been only cold and without laughter. He did not touch her, made no motion of warmth toward her. He sat on the chest and let her stand, waited for her to speak. When she could not find her voice, he said irritably, "Why did you come here?" He looked at her with distaste. "I heard once from a trader that my youngest sister was pregnant in sin and made worthless to our father. I suppose *that* is the child you brought with you, the bastard fruit of your dallying."

"I brought my child. His name is Ramad."

"I heard the child's father took himself off and left you on your own. I'll not ask how you have lived for nine years. I do not want to know. Why do you come to Burgdeeth?" he repeated.

She stared at him, her fury mounting.

"Answer me, girl! Why did you come to Burgdeeth? One does not cross that plain for the pleasure of the ride!"

"I am here because I want a new land," she lied. "Because I was tired of the rule of Seers, of living under Seers! And I left our father before that because I was tired of being groomed like a prize ewe to increase his hoards of gold!" Theel's eyes narrowed, studying her. She looked directly back at him. A lie mixed with truth, Gredillon had taught her, was the lie that would best be believed. "I wanted to bring my child to a place of freedom where he would not live under Seers! I want to be a part of something new, of a new land. I will be no bother to you. I will not even claim to know you if you like."

"That is not necessary, or possible. However, you must make your own way here. No woman has ever come to Burgdeeth without a man." He smiled dryly. "There are no unattached women here—except the slave women. And Venniver takes those as it pleases him. The guards—the guards get lonely sometimes." He looked her up and down appraisingly. "I'm sure the guards will find you more palatable than slaves, my sister—if only because you are cleaner."

She stared at Theel with fury and wondered why she had ever thought he would help her.

"There is only one set of rules in Burgdeeth. Venniver's rules. If you are to stay here, you will mark those rules well."

"I will mark them well," she said stiffly, her whole being rebelling.

Her meeting with Theel left her distraught and unnerved. She guessed she had counted on his support more than she realized. Well maybe Theel would change his superior attitude. All by Venniver's rules, was it? And as for the guards, if they thought she was fair game, they had better think again. She wasn't wasting her time on guards.

She did not go back to the storeroom, but boldly out the front door of the Hall into the street and, holding her head high in spite of her bloodstained, mended tunic, walked the length of it, past guards, past slaves working at a stone wall. She surveyed the half-finished buildings coolly, as if no one at all turned to stare at her. There was not another woman in sight. It was strange that so many buildings were incomplete, their roofs still open to the sky, so few occupied by craftsmen and their families. She saw no children. She walked to the end of the cobbled street, to the open place that Dlos had said would one day be the town square. Now it was only a morass of mud and piles of timbers and stone. The long earthen mound behind it seemed to mark the end of Burgdeeth, for beyond that the plain began, broken only by the grove of trees to the left of the mound, where she could see a guard tower rising. She knew there was a pit on the other side of the mound where a bronze statue was being cast by slaves —by Skeelie's brother Jerthon, Skeelie had told her with pride. A bronze statue that would be as tall as six men would stand one day in the center of the square. Venniver didn't do things by half. She wanted suddenly to see it, but too many guards were watching her. She could not bring herself to walk that long way around the mound in the mud to where slaves were working and perhaps risk the guards' challenge. She turned instead back toward the Hall.

As she turned, she saw Venniver himself come out of a side street with half a dozen guards and start in her direction. She felt exposed; her jaunty assurance left her, and she hurried along to an alley that joined the square and up between the buildings. She thought that Venniver watched her. He was a big man, who dwarfed the guards. Wide of shoulder, with curling black hair and beard and a strange litheness of step. His image burned in her mind long after she turned away. She thought of Theel's arrogance, and smiled. Maybe she would show Theel a thing or two about how to gain acceptance in Burgdeeth.

She found her way back to the storeroom and went directly through to Dlos's room, where she borrowed a small mirror from the old woman, and some perrisax soap. She studied Dlos appraisingly. "Dlos, I can't wear this tunic, it—the bloodstains wouldn't come out. It's so patched from the sword tear, it . . . Do you have something that I could make into a dress?"

Dlos surveyed her in silence. At last she said, "I suppose I do. What sort of thing? Coarsespun, I imagine. Very plain. You'll be working in the sculler, maybe serving in the Hall." She opened a chest at the foot of her bed, removed several worn garments, and lifted out a faded coarsespun dress. "If you take this in a little, I think. . . ."

Tayba held it up. It was very ordinary, not at all what she had in mind. "This—this will be. . . ." She lifted her eyes to Dlos, waiting.

Dlos sighed. "All right. All right." She rooted again and handed out a length of amber wool as soft as down. Tayba unfolded it, and it ran like water through her hands.

She hugged Dlos quickly and fled before Dlos could change her mind.

Dlos bent to close the chest, grumbling at Tayba's departing figure, "You had best be careful, my girl." But Tayba did not hear, nor would have heeded, her.

She found the scissors Skeelie kept in the storeroom and began to measure and lay out the fine wool. And late that night she sat peacefully sewing, as she watched Ram's quiet sleep. He had grown much better. She rose several times to touch his cheek and cover Skeelie, who slept flung out every which way across her cot.

Much later she heard the wolves howl on the mountain. Ram stirred and muttered, rolled to face the window and reach out. She wanted to pull his hand back, tuck it under the covers out of harm's way. But instead she drew the shutters closed, shivering. The wolves were not good for Ram. Why did he yearn for them so, even in sleep? She wished he had never heard of the wolf bell. Recalling the slinking jackals on Scar Mountain, Tayba saw their faces superimposed over the wolves' faces and felt fear for Ram. Gredillon had been wrong—very wrong—to train him to the use of the bell and its dark powers. She was glad the bell was lost.

"You'd think," she said to Skeelie the next day as they peeled vegetables in the sculler, "you'd think that Venniver—that he would just let us know we can stay. . . ."

"Why should he?" Skeelie countered, dumping peelings into a bucket for the chidrack. "The longer he waits, the more—you will be afraid of him and obedient to him when he does decide to speak to you."

She stared at Skeelie.

"Oh, he'll let you know, you needn't worry. In his own good time."

"How do you—how do you know what he'll do?"

Skeelie looked at her oddly. The thin child was strung tight with intensity. "I know—because I hate him. My brother is Venniver's slave. My people. . . . Ever since I was four, I've watched Jerthon slave for him, seen Jerthon beaten, felt Jerthon's hate for him. I know Venniver very well." Skeelie looked older than her twelve years; spoke with a hatred that was mature and cold. It made Tayba hesitate in what she planned—and yet, the slaves' problems were not her problems.

And the slaves were strong, healthy people. Were Seers. Couldn't they have found some way, in all these years, to escape Venniver if they had really tried? She looked at Skeelie and saw her face go closed suddenly, her eyes expressionless.

"How—how is it that he lets *you* go free, Skeelie?"

"I keep out of his way. He—he doesn't see much of me." She was peeling the roots so violently, Tayba was afraid she would cut herself. "When Venniver captured us, Dlos told him I was too little to be locked in the slave cell all day with no one to take care of me."

"And he *listened* to her? But I would have thought . . . ."

"He listened because once she saved his life. He—he

58

had gone up into the mountains. He didn't return. Dlos —knew where to look. She led three guards there. They found—found him trapped where a boulder had rolled across a cave. It took all three men to move it."   -

"But how did she . . . ?"

"No one . . . she said she had been up the plain picking herbs and heard the rumbling, that she—she thought she knew where it was. The guards said—I heard them talking once—that it must have been an earthquake. And that there were wolf tracks around the boulder—as if the wolves had come down tracking him. . . ."

Three old women bustled into the sculler with baskets of tervil and roots. Tayba and Skeelie stilled their talk, became absorbed in their vegetables.

Old Poncie pushed back her sparse white hair and glared at Skeelie, handed out a pail in her thin clawlike hand. "Here, child, take this pail and get us some water! Oh my, you've used this other bucket for scraps! *Can't you. . . .*"

Skeelie grinned at Tayba and went out swinging the two buckets. Tayba looked through the open window and saw Ram run to join her as if he'd been waiting. He looked fine and healthy now, as if he had never been sick. Behind her the old women began to whisper; she heard her name, could feel them looking at her, caught words that angered her. Well she'd rather work at serving table in the dining hall than with this whispering handful of biddies.

THEY WERE AT SUPPER in the storeroom, Ram and Skeelie and Tayba, when Venniver came to look them over like some kind of new livestock. Ram knew he was coming and bristled, stopped eating and felt almost sick, the food nauseating him. Skeelie disappeared at once behind some barrels. Ram sat stiff and apprehensive as Venniver pushed open the outside door to stand silent, blocking out the moons, a dark blotch. They could not see his face, and when he did not move or speak, Tayba began to fidget. Ram wished she would hold still; her nervousness both annoyed and amused Venniver.

Still, the sense of him was so powerful Ram could un-

59

derstand her feelings. She could not continue to eat casually under the man's steady, hidden gaze. She received the sense of him very surely, and Ram wondered, not for the first time, why she could not bear to accept, even in her private thoughts, that she had Seer's skill. She hid from the idea utterly, turned from it in terror, and he could not understand that in her.

When Venniver stepped into the room at last, so the candlelight touched his face, Ram saw Tayba's surprise. The man's cold blue eyes and curling black hair and beard seemed strange against the clear, pink-cheeked complexion, rosy as a girl's. He seemed too big for the room. Ram felt Tayba's thoughts careening like a shrew in a cage, awed by him and frightened—yet drawn to him. She began to fiddle with her plate, and Venniver looked at her coolly, gave a snort of disgust that dismissed her entirely, and turned his attention to Ram.

He stared at Ram piercingly. He was a frightening man. Ram looked back at him steadily, unflinching, with a calmness that took a good deal of concentrration.

"Ram—Ram has not been well," Tayba said nervously. Ram wished she would keep still. "He is strong, he will be a strong worker. He was sick because he fell, you can see the lump, but he. . . ." Ram stared at her, trying to make her be still. "We—we came to Burgdeeth," she said more calmly, "to be away from Seers. Perhaps Theel told you that. I—I am a good worker. We both are." She looked back at him steadily now.

"What can the *boy* do?" Venniver said mockingly.

"He—he can learn to lay stone. He will grow to be a man well-trained to the work of the town."

Venniver snorted.

Tayba looked down, keeping her hands still with great effort; when she looked up, she quailed anew before Venniver's piercing gaze. "We have nowhere else to go," she said softly. "We—we are at your mercy here."

Ram was sickened at her submissiveness. She had nearly dissolved before Venniver.

When Venniver turned to leave, he looked back at her unexpectedly and spoke much as Theel had spoken.

"You may stay here if you work as you are directed.

We have no food for idlers or for women and children who do not know their places. That means that you will keep our sanctions, both of you. There will be no favors because your brother is my lieutenant. You will hate the evils of Ynell, you will hate the Children of Ynell as I hate them. You will, if you value your life, young woman —and *his* life," he added, jabbing a careless thumb toward Ram. "If I am displeased with you, I will send you to die on the plain. I have no qualms about doing so." His look chilled Ram utterly. In one motion, then, he was gone into the night. The moons shone coldly through the empty doorway.

They stared after him in silence. "He means," Ram said at last, "that you must hate the Seers, Mamen. That is what the Children of Ynell are. That is what I am."

"Yes." She drew him to her, and he let her hold him. He could feel her discomfort at the man's cruel coldness. When she parted his hair to be sure the roots had not shown before Venniver, Ram turned his head away. And he stared up toward the mountain with a terrible need suddenly, a longing to go there, to be among the silent, pure strength of the wolves and away from the emotions that flooded and twisted around him like shouting voices.

Chapter Four

SKEELIE WAS STEALING iron spikes from the forgeman. Ram watched her in his mind, saw her slip behind the man as he worked at the forge, slip out of the forgeshop to pile the spikes in the alley. Ram kept his mind closed from her, sneaked up behind her, surprising her so she nearly cried out, his hand quick over her mouth to silence her. She was clever as a house rat at stealing. They grinned at each other, froze as a guard went by the end of the alley, then together they carried the spikes around behind the town to the pit and down into it when the guard was turned away.

Nightmarish objects peopled the pit, parts of horses cast in bronze: heads, bodies, wings. But not nightmarish when you looked. They were beautiful, the wings sweeping and graceful, the horses' faces filled with a wonder and exaltation that made Ram stare.

Jerthon turned the forge fire, his tunic and red hair dark with sweat. His eyes roved above the pit. He watched the guard walk away, assessed the one guard in the pit who slept against a pile of timbers, then gestured toward a heap of stone. The children slipped the spikes into a space between the stones, then Skeelie clung to Jerthon. Jerthon gave Ram a quick wink and hugged his little sister close. Ram could feel their warmth and closeness. It made disturbing feelings in him. Jerthon said, "The visions are not so bad now? You are learning to control them, Ram?"

"Thanks to you. I didn't—I didn't know how much I hadn't learned, until—until you showed me. The deep blocking, the turning away from the Pellian Seer's force. He is strong, Gredillon could not show me how strong— maybe even she didn't know. It has helped to learn to turn away, and yet not seem to turn. . . ." He looked at his teacher quietly. They had come very close, and quickly, when Ram lay so ill—possessed by the Pellian Seer. It had seemed a miracle the first time he had felt the touch of Jerthon's mind helping him, supporting him, when he had thought he was all alone against the Pellian.

Jerthon said, "I can only help to teach you, it is you who does the hard work." His green eyes searched deep into Ram's. "Be careful, Ramad of Zandour. Be careful of the Pellian Seer, of how you deal with him. He would kill you—he *can* kill you with that power if you waver. . . ."

"Yes. But I must learn from him—you know I must. I will be careful, Jerthon." Ram searched Jerthon's face. "Only by letting him try to mold me can I . . . can I learn to better him. There is something hidden. Something I cannot touch. The Seer quests after something, even besides controlling the power of the wolf bell. He has a great need for it and has no idea where to look. It —it has nothing to do with me, but if I could—if I knew what it was, and where. . . ." The sleeping guard stirred suddenly, and at Jerthon's silent command the children scrambled up out of the pit and disappeared into the alley, were away quickly from that warm touch with him. He took her small, bony hand. Could feel Jerthon's satisfaction in their silent, hasty retreat. When the guard slept again, they came out to walk innocently along the edge of the pit, just to be near Jerthon. They could see part of the wooden model of the statue, a full-sized carving Jerthon had made from which he now cast the bronze pieces. It rose behind piles of stone and timbers, its lifting wings catching at the wind as if the god and the two horses would lift suddenly and fly. It thrilled Ram, that statue, gave him a sense of wonder and space that held and excited him. He gazed down at it, standing there among the rubble of the pit, "Why must Jerthon work in a pit? It's so—well he is private and sheltered I guess, but —oh, I see. To block the forge fire from the north wind."

"That, but mostly to hide the work from any chance travelers. Beyond the mound, you can't see into the pit. Venniver is secretive about the statue, about the religion he plans for Burgdeeth. He doesn't want questions asked.

He just wants to do things his way with no one outside knowing. He—he says that when the stone and timbers are all moved out one day, the pit will be a root garden for winter food. Maybe it will. . . ." she said doubtfully. "That is a Moramian custom and not a Herebian's way."

"Where did he come from?"

"Venniver? From the hills along the Urobb, I heard. Down near to Pelli. He—" She turned to stare at Ram. "He has Seer's blood, Ramad. He cannot use it, except to block. But it makes—it makes a fear and a hatred in him. Something—something twisted in him. He's afraid; he's afraid of the dark mountains and what lies in them. He's afraid of the wolves. There is evil in him, and he thinks the wolves there on the mountain know and would stop him from building this town if he angered them. He thinks they prowl here at night to watch him."

Ram stared at her. Did the wolves know about Venniver? Did they care? He could not tell. He could reach out to them, but the touch was often faint and unclear. Only his terrible stress in running from EnDwyl and the Pellian Seer had made a force that drew them so strongly. "I must go there," he said quietly. "The power of the bell, of what is in me is stronger close to them. I want to be there on the mountain with Fawdref. He—he comes when I am afraid. But I want just to be near him."

"He was there helping—in your mind—when the gantroed almost killed you."

"Yes. And so was Jerthon."

The gantroed had risen dark in Ram's night visions to twist writhing around him, its coarse hair patched and scurvy; had coiled thick as five men, tall as a hill, its curdling cry shaking the air in waves around it. In his vision Ram had fled without volition, heedlessly trampling the living bones of men beneath his feet, careless of their screams as ribs and fingers were torn apart; and the gantroed pursued him so close its fetid breath sickened him. But then at last he could trample those dead-living bodies no longer, could not tolerate their pain, and had turned to face the gantroed; and had felt the Seer's wrath when he chose to challenge the monster. He had brought every power within him against the looming worm, knowing this was not a dream, that he could die at the Seer's hands, suffocated in his own bed from HarThass's dark powers. One tendril snaked along his face cold as death. Jerthon and the wolves had been with him, pushing the gantroed back, forcing the worm until at last it recoiled. But Ram knew that he must become strong enough to defend himself alone.

Yes, Jerthon whispered in his mind. *But be patient, Ramad of Zandour. The learning takes patience.*

Skeelie looked at him, puzzling. "What is it you must do? That you know in your dreams you must do?" Her eyes held his as she pushed back a thin wisp of hair. "Where must you go, Ram?" She was only a little taller than he; he would catch up to her soon. "It is the mountain. But it is more than the wolves calling you."

"I—I must go to the mountain. Yes, more than the wolves. I don't know what. . . ." He felt it in him like a voice, something pulling from the mountain, something there in the Ring of Fire, heavy with urgency.

TAYBA'S FIRST NIGHT serving table in the dining hall left her frustrated and confused. She had worn the amber gown. The light apron hid very little of its clinging ways. She had bound her hair on top her head, had, Dlos said, overdressed herself. But she'd paid no attention to Dlos. "You are there to put food on the table, not to advertise your charms. He'll know right away what *you're* after."

She wished afterward she had worn the coarsespun. Venniver's eyes had shown cold amusement, and she'd known that Dlos was right. Her anger made her so clumsy she had spilled a tray of brimming ale mugs over three guards, drenching them, and had felt Venniver laughing at her; had been too ashamed to look in his direction.

She had gotten through the night at last, embarrassed and chagrined, to return thankfully to the storeroom. She wriggled out of the amber wool and tried to sponge the stains from it, then stood staring out the window until the wind became too cold to bear. She crawled into bed cross and uncomfortable and lay hearing the guards again, shouting as the ale spilled over them.

Unable to sleep, she flung on her cloak and began to

pace. She glanced at the sleeping children and was glad they were not to awake to see her helpless rage. She stared out at the night and the empty plain, watched clouds scud coldly across the moons. What stupidity had brought her to this forsaken place? She and Ram were only strangers here, no one cared how they felt or what happened to them.

I was a stranger to EnDwyl, too, she thought suddenly. He never cared for me. I was only some virgin he could ruin in a huge joke and laugh about in the drinking halls later. And I am nothing more in this place. Nothing. I mean nothing to anyone.

Well, Ram and I have each other, she thought with defiance.

But even that thought was uncomfortable, for there were things Ram needed more than he had ever needed Tayba. *I don't need anyone! We are born alone and we are always alone and we don't* need *anyone else!*

She stiffened as Ram cried out, thrashing wildly and tangling his covers; she heard the wolves then, high on the mountain. Skeelie rose to go to him, calmed him, felt his face and gave him water; knelt there uncertainly then slipped back to bed at last. Tayba pulled her cloak closer and went to sit beside his cot. His face was warm; he was worse again, and so suddenly. She sat puzzling. The wolves howled again, chilling her. Ram stirred, then struck out at something in his dreams, his hand grazing her.

The wolves did this to Ram. It had been the wolves that sickened him before. He had been well, and now they had begun to howl again in the night and again he was feverish. She hated them. Why didn't they leave him alone?

She thought briefly that it might not be the wolves stirring him so, that it might be the Pellian Seer reaching out. But she didn't believe that. What good would it do for a Seer to reach out and sicken him? If the Pellian wanted Ram, why didn't he send a band of warriors for him? This made her shudder; if such happened, would Ram see them coming in time to escape?

Surely he would. Surely.

No, this thing that stirred him and made him reach toward the mountain even in sleep was the wolves; the wolves howled, and he stirred and became restless. And if he should go to them, she thought shuddering, he would be helpless without the wolf bell. They could kill him. She touched his face and straightened his covers, pulled away some straw that was tangled in his dark hair. Well, she would not let him go up to the mountain. She would keep him from the wolves somehow.

IN SLEEP RAM FELT HER TOUCH but was swept away into darkness; and something shone out from the dark. Paths of silver crossed in a giant web. In the center, a silver spot grew larger. He fell spinning toward it. The silver grew, was a robed figure; the Seer HarThass, his arms raised, his face hidden in darkness beneath the silver cowl. Ram tried to turn away and could not move. The silver skeins bound his feet, and began to grow into snakes.

The Seer grew taller. He threw back his cape and still his face was darkness. The web of snakes was crushing Ram. The Seer cried, *"Save yourself if you will! Save. . . ."* Seven naked men stood in the blackness, each with a knife raised to the next, terrified and waiting for Ram to direct them. *"Save yourself!"* The Seer showed him blood and pain, and Ram knew what he must do. The silver snakes were so tight around his chest he could not breathe. He tore at them helplessly.

"Save yourself or die, Ramad of Zandour! Make them kill!"

"I won't!"

But he struggled for breath, and then in utter terror he willed one man to slash the next. Blood flowed; and his bonds were loosed at once. Quickly they grew tight again, and again Ram made one man cut the next. Again the bonds loosed.

"Make them kill, Ramad! Make them kill, if you would live."

"No! No!" And he felt Fawdref then, the dark wolf grown immense to loom up before the Seer, felt Fawdref's power lashing out with his own . . . and he woke.

Woke in the storeroom seeing Skeelie bent over him,

seeing his mother, Dlos, their faces harsh with concern. Saw their relief as he reached to touch Mamen's face. He tried to speak and could not, felt the Seer pulling at him still, felt the cold cloak of oblivion waiting so close. Felt Fawdref standing guard; then felt Fawdref waver, his power slacken as the Seer of Pelli brought the power of his apprentices too, down against Ram; felt Jerthon there standing with Fawdref, both locked against the Seer's cold darkness.

TAYBA TOUCHED HIS FACE; it was like fire. Dlos began to wrap him in cool, damp cloths. They were all touching him as if they could pour life into him from themselves. Skeelie whispered, "He is pulled so far away. He . . . I can't. . . ." She reached to take Tayba's hand; and when their hands linked Tayba could see a dark vastness and see Ram spinning in its vortex as in a black river where time had no meaning. He was tumbled to a shore where the bones of dead men rose and walked.

Skeelie's vision vanished. Tayba turned away shuddering. The little girl knelt there terrified for Ram. Even with Jerthon to help him, with Fawdref, the tides of power he touched were so dangerous. Skeelie put her arms around him, wept against him and could not stop.

But when Ram woke the next morning he was quite well, as if he had never been sick. He said to Skeelie, "I am going up into the mountain." They were alone, she having brought him mawzee cakes and fruit.

"But—all right. But why are you?"

"There is something there, Skeelie. A wonder is there. Something—something of terrible importance. Fawdref knows. He would show me—but when he tries to, the Seer of Pelli sees, too. I will go up among the great wolves where the power of the bell will be strongest. Then—then I think I can block the Pellian's Seeing."

"I will steal the bell for you. I know where it is."

Ram said smugly, "I already have." He drew the bell out from beneath his blankets. "I got it this morning before anyone was awake. That old chest—Dlos has everything in there." He felt comforted, very sure, having the wolf bell near.

68

"Why didn't you take it before? Wouldn't it have helped against HarThass?"

"I expect so. But HarThass wanted me to have the bell, wanted to make me do his bidding with the bell."

"Ram, I don't understand. Why hasn't HarThass sent soldiers to capture you and take you to Pelli. Wouldn't he. . . ."

"He thinks—he thinks to train me so well I will come to him on my own," Ram said, smiling. "It has become a game with him. Oh, he will send soldiers if . . . when he finds he can't train me so. But not yet. He is like a hunting cat with a small creature, teasing it." He grinned, winked at her. "Well, that small creature can turn around and bite. Only he doesn't believe that will happen."

They left Burgdeeth in late afternoon, thinking they would not be missed so quickly if all Skeelie's chores were finished so no one would look for her.

"Dlos wouldn't care," Ram said.

"No, but your mother would. She doesn't want you on the mountain. But she won't follow us though. I—I didn't bring a waterskin," she said hastily. "There's water on the mountain and in the caves, Dlos told me."

"How does Dlos know about the mountain? No one goes there."

"Dlos's husband was a Seer. He told her."

"A Seer? But he. . . ." Ram stared at Skeelie. "I never —I've never seen that in her mind. How come he was *here*? A slave?"

"No, he was Venniver's spy. He was the man who taught Venniver to shield his thoughts and helped him come unseen on Jerthon and Drudd and our other Seers and capture us. I was only small, but later Jerthon showed me how it was. You didn't . . . Dlos blocks very well. I suppose she learned it from him."

"But he—I can't believe that Dlos—she wouldn't have. . . ."

"She knew what he did." Skeelie pulled her cloak closer against the sharp breeze. "Dlos loved him in spite of his treachery. She couldn't stop what he did. I think she—she was almost relieved when Venniver killed him. They had disagreed about something, and Venniver grew angry and killed him. She felt—it's awful to say, but she felt he was better dead than a traitor, selling his own people into slavery."

"Still she loved him though," Ram said.

"Yes."

Ram frowned. "That is why Dlos has such sadness. Her humor is all on top, hiding the sadness."

The shadows spread out from the boulders in dark misshapen pools. It was a game to slip from one shadow to the next and keep boulders between them and Burgdeeth. Ram said, "What do you mean, Mamen won't follow us? If she finds me gone, she. . . ."

"She won't come this night."

"Why not? Oh yes, she will. You don't know how she hates the wolves. What *are* you grinning about?"

"She won't come tonight, Ram."

"You're shielding. Why are you shielding? What. . . ."

She was grinning fit to kill and wouldn't let him in. At last she said, her face reddening, "She won't come this night. She'll be busy with Venniver. He is planning a supper for two, in his chambers."

He frowned, turned away, and was painfully embarrassed. "I see." At last he turned to look at Skeelie. "How do you know? You can't—Venniver is nearly impossible to See! His mind is—he blocks. You can't. . . ."

She seemed to find it all very funny. "I didn't *See*. I overheard him in the corridor. I was—borrowing—some linens from the cupboard. They don't give the slaves *anything!* And I heard him telling old Poncie what to make for supper and how to serve it and . . ." she fell into a fit of laughter, ". . . and to bring new, scented candles. Oh my, how elegant. She won't follow us tonight, Ram."

He didn't think the thing so funny. "How do you know it's for *her?* Maybe a slave—"

"He doesn't have special supper for slaves," she said. "You have to admit, he has looked at her. You told me yourself you caught his thought once and. . . ."

"Yes. All right."

"And she. . . ."

70

"All right!" He was really angry. "She must have been busy these last three nights. Parading herself."

"Yes. And he was busy looking."

They left the plain and began to climb between steep black cliffs, a narrow way that would lead to the heart of the mountain. Ram could feel the sense of the wolves, knew they were waiting.

And he could feel another power well beyond this mountain, somewhere in the sea of wild peaks that spread out into the unknown lands. A power that made him stare off toward those lands, wondering and eager.

THEY HAD BEEN SCRUBBING DOWN the sculler and kitchen, Tayba and two old women. The other three had taken sick and, she thought crossly, were probably lying in luxury in their beds listening smugly to the clank of buckets. She was sweating from the hot water. Tendrils of damp hair hung in her face. She had slipped out twice to look for Ram, wanting him and Skeelie both to help, and had found neither. The kitchen smelled of lye soap. They must start supper soon. Where had Ram gotten to? He wouldn't hide from work. Nor would Skeelie. She couldn't understand her unease, like a voice whispering. As if she knew something, but did not know it. *It is nothing. They are all right. What makes me so edgy? It's nerves. Stupidity.* But when Dlos came with clean rags and she had not seen them either, Tayba began to listen to the voice.

"Not anywhere, Dlos? Not near the pit?"

"I was just there. They're all right. What could happen to them?"

"They could go to the mountain," Tayba breathed softly, staring across at the two old women. "They could—Dlos, I know he has!"

Dlos studied her. "And what if he did, child?"

"They—the wolves made the sickness in him. I am going after Ram! I am going up the mountain!"

"You cannot go alone, you wouldn't know where to search," Dlos said scornfully.

"Yes I. . . ." She saw Dlos looking past her, and turned.

Venniver was standing in the doorway. He came into the kitchen. "You will clean yourself up," he said quietly. "Dress yourself in something besides that coarsespun. I don't want to dine with a kitchen drudge. Poncie will prepare our supper." He glanced toward Poncie, who smirked. "Well, get moving woman, dress yourself in something pleasant to look at, *you* know you're to take supper with me! What are you doing scrubbing the kitchen!"

"No one told me—Poncie said—"

"*I* don't care what Poncie said. *I'll* deal with *her!* Now. . . ."

She tried to speak calmly and could hear the tremor in her voice. "Please." She drew herself taller. Of all nights for Ram to wander off. "Please—my child is lost. I must find him. I will take supper with you tomorrow night. Willingly." The two old women, who had scuttled into a corner, began to giggle.

"*Lost child!* What do *I* care for a *lost child!*"

"Just—just for tonight. I would rather be with you. He's out there alone in the night. I can't. . . ."

Scowling, he pulled her close, hurting her, stared at her with fury. She looked back at him directly. "I will not be pleasant company tonight, Venniver." She held his eyes, willing him to listen. Why tonight of all nights? Why had Ram . . . just when Venniver had finally noticed her. "Let me go to find my child," she breathed, "and tomorrow night I will come to you, Venniver."

"I care nothing for any child. I care nothing for your problems." His fury terrified her. But then suddenly he seemed really to see her. A cold smile touched his lips. "But I care for a woman with enough spirit to say no to me. I'm sick to death of silly, terrified females," he said, glancing in the direction of the slave cell. "All right, go on, woman! Get yourself out of here!" He spun toward the door, leaving her free.

"Wait!" she said evenly.

He turned back, his eyes burning through her.

She swallowed, then said boldly, "I want a horse. I want a horse to use, to search for Ram."

"You want—*what?*"

72

"I want a horse to search for my child. I will need a horse to cover any ground, to find Ram, to keep from getting lost in the night."

"Great fires of Urdd!" He turned back toward the hall. She stared after him, her courage sinking. He would leave her there unanswered, defeated. Behind her old Poncie laughed quietly and cruelly. Tayba stood clenching her fists, then heard him bellow suddenly, "Mardwil! Mardwil! Get this wench a pack animal. Be quick about it! Put a saddle on it and bring it around to the sculler!"

She went weakly out of the kitchen, the taste of bile coming in her mouth. She hurried through the sculler into the storeroom, searching for Dlos.

Dlos was in her little room kneeling before the painted chest that stood at the foot of the cot, her short hair askew, her square, wrinkled hands hastily replacing folds of linen and wool—she seemed not to be thinking of Ram at all. She looked up at Tayba. "It is not here."

"What is not? This is no time to—"

"The wolf bell," Dlos said. "Ram has taken the wolf bell."

There was a long silence while Tayba stared at her. The wolf bell? But he could not have taken it from here. It had been lost on the plain—or EnDwyl had. . . . And then she understood. "Oh! It was you! *You* took the wolf bell from Ram. You—"

"I took it from the child where he lay beside the river. I hid it in this chest, but Ram—Ram is a Seeing child."

"The wolves . . . Ram could be dead by now."

"The wolves will not harm Ramad. They will not harm one who holds the power of the bell."

"What do you know about the bell? You can't be certain. Ram's only a child. And look how sick he's been. The wolves caused his illness, they . . . maybe they *made* him come to them."

"The wolves caused no illness. And they will not harm Ramad. Ram is more than a child, young woman. There are things you cannot deny such a one as Ram."

"Perhaps," Tayba said, unable to cope with her. The guilt Dlos made her feel was ridiculous, she had no reason to feel guilt. "I must go after him," she said shortly, turning away toward the door.

"I will go with you."

"There is only one horse."

Dlos stared at her angrily. "How would you know where to search, alone up there! Not that search is necessary. However, perhaps it will do you good to face those wolves, young woman! Now if you can get one horse, however you managed, you can get another."

So when Mardwil brought the pack pony, Tayba went back with him and helped him saddle another, against his will. "Venniver said only one," the man grumbled.

But she defied him, got the horse at last and led it back to the sculler, where Dlos had the first animal's pack tied on and was already mounted. She tied on her own pack, and soon they were above the town. Dlos said, "How *did* you manage to get horses, young woman?"

"I asked Venniver for them," Tayba said quietly.

Dlos stared at her, then looked away.

They could hear the river far on their left. The horses wanted to move slowly in the dark and shied at the looming boulders. Dlos slapped her mount and dug in her heels, and the animal settled into a pulling trot. Dlos handled her horse well, seemed to know what she was about. It was like the old times with Gredillon, when the older woman had taken charge and Tayba had only to follow. Gredillon had said once, with fury, "You must learn to do for yourself, girl. You can't expect to follow someone else all your life." Tayba had been tempted to reply, *I did for myself to get away from my father, to keep from being sold like a prime ewe, didn't I?* But she had thought better of that remark.

Now she eased herself up off the jarring trot, with one hand on the horse's withers, and looked ahead to where Ere's moons threw a wash of light across the peaks above them. They were making good time on the rough ground, would be among the peaks soon. The air grew colder, the wind cut down at them. Fissures on the mountain shone black as the moons rose higher. She pulled her cloak tighter around her. Where was Ram in this black night, in the immensity of those mountains?

74

Dlos kicked her mount into a gallop across a flat, unbroken stretch, and they pulled the animals up at the far edge to rest among boulders. The jagged peaks rose directly above them, dark with shadow. Wolves could be watching from anywhere. Tayba watched Dlos dismount and hobble her horse, then did the same, for the horses could go no farther up the steep, narrow ways. Tayba thought of climbing into that mountain on foot and shivered. "Who's to say the wolves won't kill the horses while we're gone?"

"No one is to say that. We must simply pray the wolves—that they will leave them unharmed."

. They began to climb in among the cliffs in shadow black as death. "There are caves above," Dlos said. "Do you have your lantern?"

"I have it." Tayba followed the sound of Dlos's footsteps until the old woman struck flint to tinder, illuminating the stone walls and low ceiling of the first cave.

Part Two

The Wolves

Chapter Five

RAM AND SKEELIE GROPED through black clefts deep inside the mountain. "We are going clear through it," Ram said. "We will come out into caves like an underground world. Fawdref is there."

"Couldn't the wolves have come and led us?"

"They lead us. It is all that is needed. The power gets . . . it grows stronger as we get closer."

They moved through passages in the stone so narrow they must walk sideways, and when they came at last to light again, they shouted with surprise and pleasure at the sudden golden rays of the dropping sun and stood grinning at each other. Such an urgent thing, the need for light, when one has moved in darkness.

They were in a part of the mountains now where no men had been for generations—not since Seers dwelled there among the gods. Skeelie sat down on a ledge and stared out at the hundreds of peaks that rose beyond, considering the desolation and the strangeness of that wild land. Ram stood looking, feeling the power of something immense pulling at him, and facing Fawdref's call. And he could sense forces meeting here in a conflict of which he knew he was suddenly the center. He could not settle, he was too eager to get on, was tight-strung and shaken.

When they did go on, they heard water falling and came into a tall cave lit by the sun's golden light. A waterfall plunged down from the ceiling into a light-filled pool, casting rippling reflections on the cave walls. The pool's breath was cool in their faces. Ram stripped off his clothes and swam, his body transformed in the lighted green depths into something pale and fishlike. Skeelie was drawn to that enticing world but was more modest. She turned her back to undress. They swam until they were numb with cold, then dressed and went on again through dark corridors and passages where only a dull gray light marked their way. In time they saw ahead dark shadows that seemed to move. Skeelie drew back, but Ram followed the silent shapes eagerly.

And suddenly the shadows were warm, huge bodies leaping all around them, wolves pouring around them, sweeping past each other to push close to them. Dark, rough-coated, huge. Their eyes glinted, they were as tall as the children's chests, twice the children's weight, their teeth like ivory swords. Fawdref pressed against Ram, and Ram clutched Fawdref in a wild hug. The great wolf grinned and licked his neck and cheek. His mate, Rhymanie, curved against Ram, her forelegs out, her head ducked, smiling up at him. He scratched her head and saw her yellow eyes laugh with pleasure.

Ram felt their power like a tide around him, and his own power seemed heightened so his pulse beat in a wild surge. Here, he was one with the wolves, linked in an ancient heritage of power and magic.

Yet something else stirred, too. Something dark in a different way from the wolves' powers. Something insidious and threatening. "The Seer of Pelli reaches out," he breathed. He brought all of himself to shield against HarThass's searching. Then he understood that the wolves had been shielding since he and Skeelie left Burgdeeth; linking with Ram's own shielding to hide this quest from the Pellian Seer. So much more came clear when he was near to the wolves. And there was so much more for him to learn, so much yet to understand, so much skill yet to master.

Beyond the rough arch where they stood, a deep underground world opened out. A softly lighted, mysterious world into which the children moved now, to stare around them with wonder, their footsteps echoing, their voices hushed. The grotto's high roof floated in mists. The farthest walls and arches were all but lost. For an instant they saw a time long past, saw gods and Horses of Eresu soaring on silent wings, saw that some of the horses carried men on their backs, saw a time of wonder when anything was possible to men. Ram felt, then, that the powers he sought had to do with this—with a time when all was open to man.

The vision vanished. The wolves led them through the grotto to another opening, through which they could see the setting sun and a grassy hill rising up steeply to meet sheer, black cliffs, which swept on up to a mountain peak. Against the mountain stood a building made by men, a black stone structure so well conceived it seemed to have grown from the mountain itself. They went out of the grotto and up the grassy bank and in between the black pillars to a great hall. The grass underfoot gave way to thick moss that carpeted the interior, running up over stone seats and creeping in fingers up the stone walls. The walls themselves were carved from the living stone of the mountain. Only the front wall, through which they had entered, was made of great blocks of black stone set by men.

The hall rose to an incredible height. The thin arches that floated high above might have been carved by men, or might not: pale stone bridges crossing back and forth thin as threads. Ram felt tremendous power here, felt the essence of all the ages of Ere gathered here and understood there were picture records of Ere's past sealed away and bark manuscripts of runes, and treasures beyond his dreams; and that he would return here someday, in some time yet to come.

The wolves led them through myriad openings in the hall, through chambers carved from the live stone in a labyrinth, flanked by huge slabs or by delicate filigrees of stone carven into the shapes of animals. The caves grew dim when the sun had set; but soon the moons rose, their light washing the stone walls and picking out caves high above that once had been sleeping chambers. And the ceiling was brilliant with motion, a moving panorama, a story told in pictures, that drew Ram as he started forward to climb to it, paying little attention to the narrowness of the steps or to the dizzy height. Six wolves went on with him and Skeelie. The rest turned back; many, Ram knew, because of waiting cubs. The steps were narrow and steep, carven into the cave walls with nothing to hold to. The height increased until the children could no longer look down without growing dizzy. Ram pushed on eagerly, for somewhere up there in the moonlit chambers at the roof of the grotto lay the answer to the question that burned in him with an intensity that nearly overwhelmed him.

He felt the Seer's probing then and spent himself blocking HarThass's seeking mind as the man quested blindly, not knowing where Ram was, or why, but knowing that an urgency occupied him. Like a scenting ferret, the Seer reached out. Ram felt his own powers strengthened by the wolves as they spread a cloud of darkness against the Seer.

When they reached the top of the grotto at last, they stood looking down that immense distance at the bridges of stone sweeping in arches below them, and at the one thin arch flung out across the grotto at their feet. Skeelie looked and was suddenly frozen with terror, unable to move, was convinced she would fall if she moved. She had not expected such fear as this, was confused and surprised at herself, was scarcely able to breathe for the fear that gripped her.

A wolf nudged her. She resisted, fear flaring into panic. Another pressed close, warm against her. She wanted to cry out.

Then the wolves began to push into her mind, into the white fear that held her. Gently, slowly they began to ease her, to take away the terror. She could feel Fawdref in her mind like some dark, happy troubador shouting out his songs, so it was hard to be afraid.

At last the drop into space was no longer horrifying. She could look down comfortably and was able to move forward again without losing her balance, even to look above her at the pictures on the ceiling, so close. The bright panorama hung above them alive with wonderful creatures, with the gods lifting in awesome flight; showed them a fierce history of Ere, showed killings and fire and destruction. Showed them a procession of gods moving out across the ceiling that spoke to Ram with such urgency that he pressed forward onto the thin bridge to follow it.

Moonlight swam in through the far, arched windows to touch the narrow span. Ram started across, afraid for a moment, then drawn beyond fear to that far wall and to the cave there. Fawdref came behind him. Ram hesitated as he heard Fawdref growl, low and menacing.

There, in the center of the bridge, something had begun to glow silver.

It grew quickly brighter, terrifying Ram, holding him poised precariously over empty space.

The Seer's cape became visible, the cowl hiding his face in darkness. He stood silently blocking their way. Ram's new terror mixed with Skeelie's terror, with Fawdref's fury. The Seer's intent was clear, Ram's death was clear if he should move forward.

FARTHER DOWN THE MOUNTAIN in the darkness of a tunnel, Dlos and Tayba stopped suddenly at the echo of a growl. Dlos turned her head, as if perhaps she heard more than a growl, looked upward toward the dark heart of the mountain. "We do not hear it, we hear a message. As we would hear a message of fear sent by a Seer."

Tayba followed Dlos's swinging lantern, now terrified for Ram. He should not have come here. Why had he? The smell of damp, cold stone had begun to nauseate her. Couldn't they go faster? How could they help Ram against wolves? She touched her sword with a trembling hand. What had the wolves done to him? If she let her mind dwell on it, the terror would overwhelm her. Her throat ached with the tenseness that gripped her. She would harbor no thought except that the wolves endangered him. Felt a voice within telling her she must battle wolves.

Then suddenly something else was there in her mind, subtle and compelling. It eased her fear for Ram, soothed her; yet she quailed before it.

THE SILVER CAPE moved on the night breeze that stirred through the grotto. Ram's fists were clenched. Moonlight

83

washed the cave, seemed to make the thin span shift sickeningly. The Seer's voice was cold.

"Go back, Ramad. Go back before you die." Cold and softly echoing, like some insidious whisper of death that could not be stilled.

Ram's voice cut suddenly across space, sharp as a blade. "You are a fool, HarThass! You had better take yourself back to Pelli. We are coming across."

"You cross and you die, Ramad of Zandour!"

Ram began slowly to walk toward HarThass across that thin span. He smiled. "Do you want me dead, Seer? Have you decided not to make a slave of me? Have you decided you do not want to rule the bell?" And with each step he drew closer to that faceless apparition, swallowing the fear that twisted inside him. "I think, Har-Thass, that you see your defeat so clearly you want to end it now. Before you must confess failure. You will end it by dying here, HarThass."

The Seer's voice rang. "You are no longer worth keeping to toy with, child of the mountain. I grow tired of you. I find your death more intriguing—death in a fall to that stone floor. Look down, Ramad. That will be your tomb, those hard rocks on which your body will lie crushed like jelly, a bloody smear on the stone and your tame dogs dead beside you!"

"It will not be *my* tomb, HarThass! What *is* there beyond this span, that you would prevent me from seeing? What is there that is so important to you, that you would give up your quest for the wolf bell forever?" Ram challenged. But his chagrin was terrible that his own blocking had failed, that in that instant when he faced the thin bridge and empty space, his fear had let the Seer slip by, let HarThass See the painted procession and know that it led to something urgent.

The Seer moved toward Ram. Fawdref growled and slipped up beside him on the narrow bridge, terrifying him, moved ahead of him lithe as a cat, to face the Seer. Ram lifted the bell, spoke its words urgently. The moonlight caught at the rearing bitch-wolf, making her seem to turn. "You are dust!" Ram cried. "You are only dust in this place, HarThass! You are bone and blood

84

only in Pelli! If you do not return there, you will be only dust there, silenced in death, Seer of Pelli!"

The silver cape shifted. HarThass's hate was terrible, a black tide that suffocated. Ram rang the bell, swallowing his terror; and a thousand bells rang, and the wolves cried out; and the Seer's fury rose as he moved forward along the span. Ram could feel his force, knew that Har-Thass could, by his very power, catapult him and the wolves into space; his force, the force of all his Seers, must be joined in this. *"You are dust, HarThass!"* Ram shouted.

And then he felt it: that other power with him, that surging of strength that bolstered his own. And the Seer paused. Ram moved forward. "You are dust, HarThass! And to dust you will return!" Ram stood pouring all of his power with Jerthon, with the wolves, into a tide that could sweep HarThass from that place.

The silver cape began to grow dimmer, the Seer's hands to fade. The Seer stepped back.

And the power within Ram lifted, Ram's own power and the power of the wolves rising with Jerthon to sweep down on HarThass so hard the Seer cried out in fury, his sudden fear vibrating across the grotto fainter and fainter still until it clung in echoes of anger.

Clung, long after he had vanished.

At last the span before Ram was empty. Then, shaken, swept with relief, the little procession began to cross the thin bridge in the still wash of moonlight, Skeelie clutching gratefully at the pale wolf that walked so carefully just ahead of her. Across the span, they could see a small cave opening. And the procession on the ceiling traveled with them toward an unknown wonder of such urgency for Ram that he was almost sick with the need to reach it.

Below them two figures looked upward, could not call out, stood watching the children and wolves cross over the high span until at last they reached a stone ledge and turned into the cave, to disappear.

Tayba swallowed, exhausted by her own emotions and by her fear. That other power, that had spoken to her— it had been with Ram up there, helping Ram. She had no sense of what it was. But she was warmed and supported by it. Her mouth tasted of metal. She felt sticky with sweat, even in this cool place. What were they doing up there? She had never imagined that wolves would climb into heights like that, like great cats. She wished they would come back, wished Ram were there on the ground beside her, would not rest until he was.

FAWDREF led the children slowly, letting them look. They both had cricks in their necks, could not stop gazing upward at the solemn procession where gods with folded wings walked solemnly beside men. The procession traveled up mountains and across valleys, was attacked by fire ogres, skirted lakes of fire. The gods could have flown in safety, yet they did not fly.

The Seer who led them carried a small carven box. And in that box lay, Ram knew, a power like nothing else on Ere, a power that excited and awed him. The gods marched out of the caves at last onto a high mountain meadow; and ahead of them across the meadow, a slim, towerlike mountain rose into cloud. "Tala-charen," Skeelie breathed. "I thought—I thought it was only a story. The mountain like a castle, with jewels and beautiful things inside. What do they . . . ?"

The last picture showed a cave high in the peak of Tala-charen, where a Seer placed the box into a wall and covered it with stone. Then the gods turned and launched themselves into space like great wild birds soaring out.

And the procession of Seers turned back down the mountain. Ram knew then that because of the caching of the box there, men and gods no longer dwelled together. Had become at the moment of its placement apart from each other. This, then, was the cause of the parting. This box that held the most powerful force in Ere. This was why he was here, this force was, he knew, needed now upon Ere. And it was in his power to release it.

They climbed at last, quite silent, down a stair in the outer wall, reached a bay halfway down where the cold night wind came in over a wide ledge. The wolves from below had gathered here onto the stones and outcroppings. The children stood looking down over the moon-washed land. A half-dozen wolves stood boldly at the edge letting the wind whip their fur and flatten their ears, then raised their voices in a wailing chorus.

"I will go to Tala-charen," Ram said. "And soon." His blocking of the Seer was stronger now—yet it was too late. HarThass had seen too much; would be an increased danger in what Ram had to do. Yet for a few moments he held a curtain against HarThass that blinded and confused the Seer. "There is need for the power the gods placed there. Was I. . . ." He stared at Skeelie, then his eyes searched Fawdref's. "Was I born to this, for this one thing, to bring the stone out into Ere?"

Fawdref's answer was shaded with meaning. He made Ram understand that no man was born to one thing. That there was no power that could make a babe come into the world for any purpose. There was only the coming together of powers and events, the linking into a whole that made time and need bring an urgency upon life. This was how he was born, a culmination to that urgency. There was no one intelligence that could dictate his birth or would presume to. If he succeeded in bringing that power out, the forces of Ere would be bent into a new pattern; if he did not . . . but Fawdref broke off and turned to stare out over the land, his mind dark and watchful.

TAYBA LAY WATCHING the morning's soft light flood the grotto, catching at the labyrinth and soaring spans; she remembered the silver-caped Seer up there last night, Ram balanced on the thin bridge, the ring of their voices echoing hollowly. She turned to see the children, already up, bringing water from a pool then burrowing in her pack for breakfast, for they had eaten all their own food. She saw Dlos crouch over the little fire against stone, to lay mawzee cakes to warm, strips of mountain meat to toast. She watched the wolves, some distance away, eating from the kill that part of the pack had brought in during the night. Even now she was fearful of them— though she understood at last that here lay Ram's safety, that they did not threaten him. She understood at last— as she should have long before—where Ram's real danger lay. Where else, she thought, wondering at her own confusion, but with the Seer of Pelli? Had her very confusion been a part of that dark Seer's twisting, insidious ways? Had he meant to use her, in some way, against Ram and the wolves? But he had not used her. Perhaps some other force had prevented that. For it seemed to Tayba that a terrible balance of forces surged and tilted around her. She wanted only to turn away from the turmoil; this was nothing she could touch or have influence over; was nothing she wanted any part of.

She rose and folded her blanket, remembered the children curled against wolves last night, sleeping in perfect safety, Fawdref's great head sheltering Ram's small head so she had lain awake a long time, watching them. She was tolerated here with the wolves, but she was not a part of this, nor ever could be. The children had played with wolf puppies around the fire last night, laughing, squealing with pleasure, and she had only been able to watch the bitch wolves in silence as they, perfectly at ease, had lain beside the human children and the cubs. I haven't the faith Ram has, she thought. Even yet, now that I know they will not harm Ram, I can't have faith like that. I am empty inside me—and I do not know why.

When they had breakfasted, they left the grotto. The wolves remained behind. The sadness of parting between children and wolves made Tayba turn away, to go on ahead into the dark, low tunnels. The children caught up at last, following the lantern light, and were very quiet.

Chapter Six

As Tayba dressed for Venniver that night, she heard the wolves high on the plain and saw again Fawdref facing her, tongue lolling in a terrible grin as if he made fun of her. She saw him sleeping beside Ram, their heads cradled together, saw the little cubs playing, snarling and chewing the children's hands innocently, tumbling, chasing Ram through the shadowed cave among resting wolves. Saw the wolves watching her, watching.

She closed the shutters so the howls were muffled, tied the throat of the amber wool, took up her cloak and went out along the back halls, past the door to the dining hall. Though the building was closed tight, the cold wind pushed in in icy streams through the ill-fitting shutters, to meet itself around her bare ankles. Doors had been left ajar, and she could see the austere rooms, impersonal as Theel's room. She supposed Venniver's would be the same, bare and rough. She faced his door, touched the thick wood slabs, and knocked. When he did not answer, she lifted the latch and stepped in—stood staring.

The room was not bare, nor austere. It was a huge, rich room, its furnishings elegant, its colors luminous. She had seen nothing like this since she left Zandour. Tapestries covered the stone walls, opulent scenes in red and garnet and amethyst like spilled jewels. The floor was strewn with mawzee straw and rushes, thick and soft to her tread. The supper table was set near the fireplace, laid with silver cutlery, and plates that must surely have come from Carriol's white-clay kilns, plates painted with flowers and birds and small animals among leaves. And the wine goblets were of silver, finely chased. The room was huge and square, heavy-raftered. A second chamber opened off it. These rooms must occupy the entire northwest corner of the Hall. They were furnished with heavy pieces of carved furniture like nothing else in Burgdeeth, smooth, polished. Ornately colored oil lamps hung from the rafters, their flickering light catching at the brilliant colors of tapestries and polished wood.

The bed was immense, tapestry covered. There were carved chests, intricately fashioned chairs; and the splendor of the tapestries laid a richness over all. She might have stepped into one of the finest houses in Ere. A room designed for an elegance of living she had not thought of in connection with Venniver—yet thought of now quite easily. It fit the man—fit him perfectly.

There was another, narrower door at the left, but she knew instinctively that Venniver was not there. She pulled it open and saw a room for private bathing, with what must be a drain to carry the wash water away, and a tall cabinet for clothes.

She closed the door and crossed the room, stopping to run her hand over a chair covered with soft hides. She tried it, sinking down deliciously—then rose quickly. This was Venniver's chair and very big, swallowing her. She didn't like the sudden sense of being possessed by it.

In the smaller of the two rooms stood a huge painonwood table with writing crock and quills, and with a row of leather-bound books at one end. Books with their own belted brass covers, each locked with a brass lock. She could imagine Venniver sitting at the table, ciphering, making up the accounts of the town, she supposed. But why would account books be so carefully locked?

She returned to the main room, found a striking stone on the hearth and lit the fire laid ready. And for no reason, the memory of the grotto filled her mind, and the dark wolves whose eyes searched hers with the intelligence of men; and an unease gripped her that took all her strength to put down.

She turned back to the fire at last, but her mind could not settle. The wolves seemed to reach, to watch her so she was not alone there. And there was something else watching, seeing too much, appraising her. She knelt quickly and flung a handful of kindling into the fire so it flared up, then rose to pace the room, scowling. Well if the room was peopled with wolves and Seers, let them see what they chose to see—she was not above being an exhibition if that was what they wanted!

Pacing, impatient now for Venniver to be there, not to be left alone with whatever forces crowded her, she stood once more before the locked books so neatly arranged. What could they contain of such importance?

Maybe one day Venniver would unlock them for her. Or perhaps she would unlock them herself.

When she turned, her hand trailing the brass binding, Venniver stood in the doorway looking at her. He moved into the room slowly, removing his cloak. "Do they interest you, my locked books?"

"They—they are beautifully made," she said quickly. "As is everything here. To find this," she said, indicating the room, then her eyes holding his, "to find all this in a city where everything else is—yet so unfinished. . . ."

"So rough."

"Yes."

He came easily toward her. "You fit this room nicely. You have an elegance, my dear Tayba—when you are dressed for it, when you have washed the grease away —that goes very nicely here. Now come and pour some wine for us." He set out an amber flask and two glasses and, while she poured, he laid aside his belt and scabbard of arrows.

And so her life became suddenly one of such contrasts as she would not have thought possible in so crude a town. If, in the daytime, she scrubbed on her knees and hoed, sweating, in the hot sun, her coarsespun scratching unbearably, nights were another matter. Then she bathed herself and dressed in something soft and entered into Venniver's opulent apartments and into his overbearing and satisfying presence.

She did not speak of this new part of her life to Ram, nor did he. She hoped he had the decency to leave her some privacy. Besides, Ram seemed, since that night on the mountain, completely wrapped in some inner life. And he seemed so much stronger and surer of himself. Once he said, in a moment of confidence and quite casually, "It is not so hard to deal with the Seer of Pelli now. Fawdref has shown me many things."

"What sort of things?"

"He shows me how to take what I want from Har-Thass and remain untouched by him." His dark eyes were inscrutable. She dared not ask him more, but prayed to the gods for Ram, then wondered what good that did and felt helpless and inadequate.

"I must take what I need from the Seer of Pelli. When the time comes that he calls me, when he commands me to leave Burgdeeth, then *I* will be the stronger and need not follow his command." He stared up at her, unsmiling. "Yes, Mamen. That is what he prepares me for— or thinks he prepares me for. To come to him. He has never ceased in that."

"But you can't—you *cannot* think to defeat him so easily. No one is stronger than the ruling Seers, Ram!"

"I do not do it easily. I work very hard at it. And I will be stronger one day."

"But if he knows what you plan. . . ."

"He does not know. I can shield from him now. And I have help in that." He looked at her steadily.

She could do nothing but believe in him and pray for him, whether the gods heard her or not.

Ram's ninth birthday came, and she caught a bird for him in the traditional Zandourian way, in a trap Dlos provided, and let him free it at first light. He stood staring after it, wish making, but too solemn, the wish having a power in it that no normal child's wish would have.

She knew Ram went to the mountain at night sometimes, and sometimes she heard the wolves' chilling voices close to the town. If Venniver woke and heard them, he would sleep fitfully and be cross and irritable the next day, so the guards, and Tayba herself, avoided him. Why did the wolves upset him so? They should be —to Venniver—only wild animals no different from foxes or stag. But he never hunted wolves, Dlos told her that, though he went out after other game.

Once he said, "They are not normal wolves. Last year I cornered one in a canyon while I was hunting stag. I meant to kill it, but. . . ." He scowled at her, seemed loath to reveal his feelings; but then he continued. "It looked at me the way a man would look. Wolves don't—ordinary wolves don't—look a man in the eye, Tayba. Never. This one did. Something—something prevented me from shooting, *made* me turn my arrow away. I wish—I wish they were not on the mountain." She felt he was not telling her all of the reason for his fear. But she did not ask Venniver questions. She only listened when he wanted to talk.

He began to give her occasional gifts from the locked trunk at the foot of the bed, then from a safe hidden beside the fireplace. An amethyst ring, a deep rose pendant. He poured out amber wines for her late at night and un-wrapped delicacies of soursugar and candied onyrood pods, treasures hoarded from his once-yearly trading in Aybil or Farr. Venniver's pampering was heady fare; brought her really alive once more, his rapt attentions so very much what she wanted, what she needed to make life seem complete.

And when he told her of his plans for Burgdeeth, his eyes burned with excitement. She marvelled at his words. He had begun this town from nothing; only the plum grove had stood here beside the river Owdneet. He thought it an omen that the grove should stand, missed by the flowing lava. An omen prophesying good for Burgdeeth.

On this site he had found stone, trees for timber, dragon bone nearby. Everything except labor; and Venniver had taken care of that, had ridden into the wild hills to the east with an army of thirty men strongly mounted and routed families there, bringing out not only good slaves, but the gold they mined. Some years later when he rode out again down the river Urobb, he had taken two dozen more prime slaves, five of them Seers. Venniver smiled "I had a Seer of my own then. A willing man with a rare skill. He could block the minds of Seers so completely they never knew we were there. He

93

died later. Died wishing he could go quicker than he did."

He told her how he had captured the slaves along the river Urobb, slitting the sentries' throats and driving the horses off to be rounded up later. "Fine horses, as fine a catch as those slaves, or nearly." He lived the battle again, lustily. "They fought well. And fought the whole night before we routed them. We clubbed and bound them—a real catch, you can pick them out. The tallest, strongest ones. They're the cleverest, too. And we have two bronze workers among them, just the thing to make the statue. That short, fat fellow, he's of passable talent, and as strong as a bull. But the tall, defiant one with the long hair, the Seer. He's a troublemaker, but he has real skill with the metal. He's worth the extra trouble—until the statue's done."

"What—what will you do with him then?"

"Kill him I suppose. He's a nuisance to have around. Sell him, maybe."

She felt a sickness grip her, then a sudden compelling desire to look at the statue, to look at Jerthon again. Felt a terrible sickness for Skeelie, who loved her brother too much. She tried to understand Venniver's pride in the ownership of men. He looked at the slaves as if they were work animals. She rose from the deep chair, nearly spilling her wine, and began to pace. She couldn't understand her own concern. For Urdd's sake, what did she care! They were only slaves. "What were they doing anyway, riding along the Urobb?" she said irritably.

"I think they were fitted out for some expedition. Seeking new land, maybe. Well," he chuckled, "they found their new land all right." He laughed heartily, and she felt a moment of revulsion, but then watched him with increased interest. His lust for living, his cruel, headlong lust in taking life, in taking what he wanted, excited her.

And when he talked about his plans for Burgdeeth, she could see the town as he did, the grandeur of the finished city. He drew her to his desk one night to show her drawings of the Set he would build south of town, a sprawling white stone building with inner gardens and fountains where a man could live as he was meant to live. A Set with a high wall around it, and a gate that could be locked. With stables to house the mounts of the army he would keep. And at the gate of the Set, a white temple of worship for the people of Burgdeeth—but with all this, still he did not show her what was so carefully locked in those brass-bound books.

The bronze god-statue would stand in the square of the town, dominating all. She stared at the drawings, hardly believing the magnificence he dreamed. His plans were as opulent, as rich, as the apartment was. A rich taste for luxury, he had. A rich taste for women, too, so he wanted her powdered and perfumed, draped her in gowns of the softest Sangurian silk. She had not been so pampered since her father's wives had groomed and dressed her, preparing her to be sold.

And he gave her the duty of taking food to the slaves, a privilege Dlos had enjoyed, though Tayba couldn't understand why it was a privilege. "You will take the supper from now on," he said. "It is part of the ritual I plan for Burgdeeth." The idea of being chosen pleased her. The actual duty did not. She did not like marching behind guards the length of Burgdeeth with the supper basket like some Moramian chattel. Well, but if Venniver wanted it. . . .

"It is an honor to carry food to the slaves," Dlos said. "But do not speak to them. The guards will report everything."

She set off several nights behind the two guards, feeling stupid and conspicuous, was glad when they entered the plum grove away from the stares of the other guards on the street, there by the brewhouse.

The ancient grove stood just beside the pit and mound. The twisted trees had been there long before Burgdeeth. How they could have escaped the ravages of the volcanoes was hard to see—unless the gods had so provided. Beyond the low cell building, the tall guard tower thrust up. Three guards lounged in its open loft, looking down. To her right was an outhouse and a washing shed with some tattered garments hung to dry.

At the door to the cell the taller guard took her basket

from her, pulled back the cloth, and lifted each item to inspect it, the five loaves, the three boiled chidrack, some kind of pudding in a crock, then jumbled them carelessly back. On the third night he stripped the meat from the leg of a chidrack with his teeth as if he enjoyed defiling the slaves' food. He stared at her insolently, a lump of meat clinging to his pale mustache, and motioned her forward as the other guard unlocked and swung open the iron door. As she passed him, he caressed her shoulder. She stepped farther into the dark cell than she had gone before, to hide her anger; and at once was caught up with curiosity.

The room was only dimly lit by the open door, and by the one tiny window at the far end. It smelled of too many people. She could see a mass of huddled figures, could pick no one out. She moved deeper into the room, wanting to see, and was stopped by the guard's clipped words. "Far enough! Hand the basket out."

She did as she was told and felt a hand brush hers as the basket was taken from her. Felt something touch her mind so she startled, caught her breath with shock. The guard pulled her away, and the door was slammed and locked. Only an instant had passed, she had heard no voice in the cell. But something had laid bare her mind in that moment, completely opened her most private self in an inspection that shocked and infuriated her.

She made her way back to the sculler unable to quell the helpless feeling of exposure. And in the sculler she dropped a plate, then stood staring at it stupidly where it lay in pieces on the stone floor.

In the past, Ram had touched her mind. The Seer of Pelli had touched it and nearly driven her mad. But nothing like this had ever invaded her. She felt betrayed; nothing, nothing had ever touched the skill in her that she feared so violently and did not want.

She dressed carefully for Venniver that night, wanting gaiety, needing to wipe away that powerful assessment of herself there in the slave cell. With Venniver, in the opulence of his presence and his attentions, she could forget the slave cell. Nothing bad could happen to her as long as she was with Venniver.

Their splendid, rich nights were broken only occasionally by the sudden chilling voices of wolves on the mountain, or wolves crying close by on the plain. Chilling howls that would goad Venniver into irritability so that he became cruel with her, frightening and angering her.

And then one night when Ere's two moons rose round and golden over the eastern hills, making all the plain shine with a pale, black-etched glow, the wolves came into Burgdeeth.

They came directly into the town and stood in the shadows, raising eerie howls that echoed between the stone walls. Doors were flung open, men shouted, candles and tapers were lit. Lanterns swung wildly in the streets, and the guards pulled bows taut; but the wolves moved so fast, were nearly invisible in the shadows. She could not believe Fawdref would come here, endangering his pack. And she was terrified for Ram, for surely Ram would rush to help them and could be shot. Cold with panic, she watched Venniver fling on his cloak and rush out; then she ran to the storeroom, terror-stricken—and found Ram gone. She returned to the front of the hall and stood shivering in the doorway trying to see, wanting to run into the night shouting for Ram and not daring.

Men were running in the street, moon-bleached then invisible as they passed through shadow.

There was squawking from the chidrack pens. But these wolves would not come into Burgdeeth to steal chidrack. A wolf howled close by, chilling her; sending a hush upon the town as men tried to locate its position; wolves were everywhere—and nowhere.

Terrified for Ram, she slipped away from the building into shadow as wolves howled from several directions: one then another as if they played games with the men. Arrows plunked against buildings as guards shot on the run, pursuing shadows. "Ram!" she whispered, wanting to scream out to him. Two wolves howled from opposite directions, drawing the men out; drawing them away from the town.

She heard a commotion above the gardens then, heard screaming as if a horse had been brought down. Wherever the wolves were, surely Ram was there. She began to run, stumbling, pulling up her skirt to keep it from her flying feet, dodging guards, hoping Venniver did not see her, keeping to shadow when she could.

She came at last around the hall to the gardens and saw black shapes of guards against the moons with bows drawn, and beyond them the leaping silhouettes of wolves. Arrows were loosed, the wolves began to run and leap in the moonlight, doubling back and forth. A second round was loosed, silver streaks—and not a wolf fell. Again the arrows sought them and missed.

Cries of disbelief rose among the men. She heard Venniver shouting and ducked back. Mounted guards thundered around the hall, and more wolves were streaming out now from the town pursued by mounted men.

Then the wolves began to retreat: those that leaped against the moons, and those that fled to join them. No wolf lay dead. Arrows silvered the ground. Venniver's men thrust forward running, bows taut, the riders overtaking the wolves and passing them.

Near to Tayba, standing in shadow, someone— *Ram was there.* Silent, intent—yet when finally she had moved to join him he had disappeared.

Something drew her eyes to the white guard tower beyond the south gardens. It rose like a shaft of ice in the moonlight, well above the grove. Was that Ram running toward the grove? She ran too, in plain sight now, unsheltered from the moonlight.

RAM HAD STOOD in the shadows, held nearly mesmerized with the strength of the force he created as he brought the vision of wolves out from within himself, as he conjured running wolves leaping before arrows that could not touch them—a dozen wolves, twenty, twice that, until Venniver and his guards were nearly mad with impotent rage, firing and firing, shouting. Then at last Ram let his phantoms retreat, watched delighted as Venniver's guards thundered after them. He felt Fawdref's cool, silent wolf laugh from somewhere the other side of town.

When Ram slipped away from behind the Hall, he knew that Tayba was standing close by, watching, not understanding what she saw any more than Venniver did. He was disgusted with her for that; she could have understood, had she wanted—had she tried. He knew she saw him, followed him. He doubled back, nearly invisible in the shadows as he moved to join Fawdref and the real wolves above Burgdeeth.

WHEN TAYBA reached the dirt mound beside the grove, she stopped. She could not see Ram. There was stealthy movement down in the pit. She crept past the mound to see, stood staring into the blackness.

There were men down in the pit, moving something heavy. Carrying long, heavy objects between them down and down into somewhere black, into deep shadow. Then guards were riding toward her, spurs rattling. She dropped down the side of the pit, skinning her leg, and lay still until they passed. She was not certain why she hid, except she could never explain her presence here to Venniver.

When it was safe to move, she stood in the pit trying to make sense of the twisted, indecipherable shapes on every side of her. She could hear movement somewhere to her right. She put her hand out to something lifting in a curve and felt metal. It looked—it was a wing; she could feel feather shapes under her fingers. Yes, an immense bronze wing. And there, she could make out the head of a horse lying against a pile of timbers. She looked up and caught her breath.

Towering above her, pale in the moonlight, rose a god. He leaped skyward flanked by two winged Horses of Eresu, almost soaring already as they rose in flight.

But they could not lift in flight yet remain poised, so still. She crept forward to reach out, hardly daring. . . .

They were made of wood. She let out her breath and found her heart was pounding.

She turned then and saw a line of men in the near dark, carrying long timbers between them. When she turned back she saw a man standing beside her, silent, so tall, his red hair loosely knotted. His eyes were full on her, terrifying her. *Jerthon!* There were sweat stains on his tunic, and his hands were scarred over with burns

99

from the smelter. She wanted, unreasonably, to touch them.

He saw what she felt about the statue. She thought he knew everything about her, and she was so shaken she thought such probing was his right. He destroyed her, lifted her—in an instant he showed her a world of wonders that elated and terrified her, showed her the real gods, lifted her in flight as the gods lifted, showed her the sense of wonder and immense sadness that belongs to the Seer; showed her more than she could grasp. They stared at each other in silence; and then it was she who turned and fled.

She felt his disappointment in her as she climbed out of the pit to safety. He had made her see visions she could not cope with, concepts quite beyond her in their vastness. She stood in the empty square hearing the wolf hunters far away and feeling so desolate and lost she thought she could not move from that place, wanted to crouch there weeping, to bury herself there and never face anything again, to die there.

She should be searching for Ram and was unable to think where to search, heard men's distant cries that meant nothing. She turned in confusion toward the hall, then stopped, staring.

The wolves stood in a circle on the plain above the hall, facing into Ram and Fawdref. The riders were drawing close to them—then Ram raised his arms, and a second mass of wolves appeared in front of the riders, running hard. The men shouted, closed the distance on straining horses, were almost up to the wolves when—the wolves vanished. Simply disappeared.

Ram's wolves seemed to smile, their tongues lolling. She saw pale Rhymannie lift her head with cool pleasure, saw Ram grin. The riders were milling, shouting; and then the phantom band appeared again suddenly in the other direction. The riders wheeled after them.

They had not seen Ram or his wolves.

The fleeing band led them a chase, then she heard shouting again and knew that, again, the wolves had disappeared.

Wolves running on the plain one minute, and gone the

next. She stood staring at Ram in awe. This child—her child; maker of visions.

He looked at her and grinned, then said softly across the night, "Yes, Mamen. Visions. Visions for our leader Venniver." And his meaning made her shudder and turn away.

Chapter Seven

"BUT I ONLY WENT into the street! You were out there, Venniver! Wolves couldn't hurt me with you there."

"Wolves were *in* the street! They could have killed you!"

"But they didn't kill me."

He stared at her with helpless fury. She had never seen him so angry. "Those wolves were devils, disappearing and—and the arrows didn't. . . ." He began to sweat. "For all I know they were straight out of Urdd, come down from the fires of those cursed mountains! You hadn't any business out there! Why were you there, you—"

"I told you! I just wanted to see, I just—you know I didn't go far into the street, you can see I scratched my leg running back, falling on the steps. . . ."

"I can see you scratched your leg." He stared at her suspiciously. "Next time—next time stay in here. I don't want you eaten by wolves."

Already it was growing light, the night gone in chasing phantoms. Old Semma had brought tea and bread and cheese. Tayba had just poured out the steaming dark brew when a guard came pounding. Venniver rose, furious, to fling open the door. "What the fracking Urdd do *you* want!"

"There are timbers missing, a whole pile of them. They were—there must have been twenty there in the pit. Not just a few this time. They—"

"*Where in Urdd do timbers go? What in the Urdd—well get out and look for them. There ought to be tracks. Get on out of here.*" Venniver slammed the door, threw on his cloak and went out. Tayba could hear a good deal of shouting and swearing outside. When he returned at last, his mood was so black he yelled at her for no reason. She snapped back at him, but was greatly amused at his fury—and quite pleased to know something Venniver did not. Though why timbers would be missing was a puzzle. "What difference does it make, a few logs?"

"The point, my dear Tayba, is who took them? And why? Where in Urdd," he said with cold fury. "Where does someone hide timbers? You don't slip timbers into your tunic! And there'll be so damned many wolf tracks and hoofprints from last night we'll never—those wolves! Those fracking damned wolves!" He stopped speaking to stare at her. "There couldn't be a connection!" he said, puzzled. He began to pace, whacking at a chair as he passed.

"Could—could the guards have miscounted, forgot someone moved them?"

"If Pennen miscounted, I'll have his ears on a stick!"

She shivered, thinking of last night in the pit, of that line of silent men carrying the timbers into shadow. What was it all about? And Ram had been a part of it, surely, had used the wolves to distract Venniver and his guards while the timbers were moved. And Jerthon—he had stood watching her so intently, had caught her unguarded, looked at facets of herself that—*that did not exist. That were none of his affair!*

Well she was certain of one thing. She was not going into that slave cell again. Not where Jerthon could study her once more. She would not subject herself to that. She watched Venniver until he stopped pacing and turned to look at her and saw her rising color. His temper faded. She said sleepily, "Must I—*must* I take food to the slaves today? It is such a bore."

He scowled. "It only takes a few minutes."

"But it—I don't like going there. It's smelly, for one thing. All those unwashed bodies. And—and I don't like the guards so—well, so familiar," she said carefully.

He stared. "What do you mean, so familiar?"

"They—it's the way they look at me," she said softly. "They—as if they're thinking things."

He roared. "That better be all they do, is look!" His

laughter was raucous. "You can't blame a man for looking—But if they do more than look. . . ."

"One did once. He touched me."

"Which one?" His fury flared, frightening her. He was suddenly, passionately, jealous.

"I don't remember which, I never look at their faces. I just walk behind them to that damnable cell. . . . Couldn't someone else take the food? Couldn't just the guards take it? Why must a woman. . . ."

"It's not a man's work; it's demeaning for guards to carry food to slaves. It's a privilege for you; it's part of the rituals of Burgdeeth, you know that. And, my dear Tayba, it is also a sign that I trust you." He took her chin, turned her face to him. "I *can* trust you, Tayba?"

She stared at him boldly. "If you could not, Venniver, what would you do?"

"If I found I couldn't trust you, my dear Tayba, I'd lock you in the slave cell."

She caught her breath; her eyes blazed with anger.

He burst out laughing. "I like you when you're angry. I like to see fight in you. You're a fiery, beautiful creature." He stared at her as if he could never get enough of looking.

Later she said softly, "May I stop carrying food to the slaves?"

"Great Urdd! Yes, all right!"

IT WAS SOME NIGHTS LATER that she stole the hidden key to Venniver's books, lit a lamp, and seated herself boldly at his desk. She didn't understand why she wanted suddenly to see what was written in those locked volumes, but she had hardly been able to wait until the sound of hooves died as Venniver and Theel rode out to hunt the stag. She had become, in the last days, obsessed with the books. Had watched him, while he thought she dozed over her wine, take the key from behind a tapestry, fit it into one of the locks, and quickly enter some accounts. She felt almost as if something unheeded inside her directed her to take up that secreted key.

She scanned dull pages of accounts, of crops and materials, until she came at last to a book marked, *Edicts and Commandments of the Gods*. She pulled the lamp closer.

Here were the laws that would rule Burgdeeth when the town was opened to craftsmen and their families come up from the coastal countries seeking a new way of life. Well, she thought, her eyes widening, they would find a new way of life all right. More than they ever planned.

Venniver had woven a whole religion for Burgdeeth to live by. Temple services, special prayers and festival days. Special taboos. Women could not touch a horse, except Landmaster's wife. There were laws of contrition, laws against all kinds of sinning. But all couched in beautiful prayers and rituals. His writing was compelling. He was clever at shaping intricate ceremonies that would fascinate men: would soothe and entrap them, make them want to obey.

Only slowly would Venniver's laws take shape. Only slowly would the religion unfold itself. But at last a generation of people carefully bred to his commandments would live in Burgdeeth. People who had made themselves slaves willingly, in the name of his religion. People who would bow before gods they thought demanded human sacrifice, before Deacons who would burn Seers, burn little children and even babies if they were born Seer, in alarming and compelling Temple rituals.

A religion of terrifying cruelty, couched in righteousness. A religion that made the birth of a Child of Ynell the mark of the whole town's sinning. A religion, she thought, that would steal over men's minds slowly, artfully, to hold them trapped in false beliefs. He painted with strong words. He was a leader few would resist, had a power that appalled and excited her.

She sat shivering, thinking of the rich web of commandments and ceremonies, then started suddenly and turned as if someone had spoken her name in the empty room, stood up and drew on her cloak, needing suddenly and desperately to be with Ram. She hurried out into the dark, empty corridor and along it to the storeroom to find a lantern lit, and Dlos bending over Ram. Tayba caught her breath, knelt beside him, shocked. He was so very white. He was awake but unaware of them.

"He woke screaming," Dlos said. "Rose up in bed flailing against something, crying out."

"What—what did he say?"

Dlos looked at Skeelie. The child's eyes were huge and frightened. She said, "He thinks—he said HarThass would see him die first. Just that." She shivered. "I don't—I can't . . ."

Tayba put her arm around Skeelie, pulled Ram tight to them, trying to warm him. "We must help him. Something. . . ." She turned to look at Skeelie. "A Seer! Could a Seer help him, Skeelie? Could. . . ." She caught her breath at her own raging madness. "Could—Jerthon?" Her hands were trembling.

"Jerthon *is* helping him," Skeelie said quietly. "Jerthon is. . . ." She stared at Tayba, searching for something in her face. "You don't—Jerthon, all our Seers, are holding against HarThass. They—it is not enough. HarThass—the powers are balanced. Only—I think only you can help now."

"But I—*I can't*. . . ." She was almost dizzy, so faint. "What—what about Fawdref? Doesn't Fawdref. . . ."

"Fawdref, all of them hold HarThass away. Even wolves need help," Skeelie said patiently. "The bell—there is power in the bell itself. You—" she was crying. "You must take the bell to the mountain. There is magic in closeness. If the bell could be close, it would draw Fawdref and Ram together, close where your own power can strengthen the bond, not here where Ram is too sick to reach out. Jerthon—Jerthon waits to see if you will do this for Ram."

"To *see*—what did he think I would do! What did he. . . ." She rose, furious, snatched up her cloak, took the wolf bell from Skeelie in a whirl of temper; did not stop to wonder what Skeelie meant about *her* power. Ran away up through the gardens, out onto the plain in the night hoping Venniver's hunt was not near, wishing she had a horse and not daring to go back. She stumbled over boulders, wrenched her leg, ran up the empty plain pulling her cloak close against the wind.

The night darkened as the moons dropped. Her sandals were torn and her foot bleeding. Anger, and fear for

Ram, flayed her on like a beaten horse until she came at last to the first peaks.

She swallowed the fear that lay like gall in her throat, and held up the bell, thought of Fawdref in a desperate, tearing cry of silence.

IN THE SLAVE CELL Jerthon, Drudd, Runnon, Pol, and young Derin sat unmoving, their evening meal untouched, every breath concentrated on quelling HarThass, on lifting Ram, holding Ram safe. Drudd's broad shoulders hugged the shadows beyond the flicking light of the candle. Little Derin, the only woman Seer among them, hunched small and nearly lost in darkness, her red hair pushed back under a knotted cloth. Jerthon scowled, feeling Tayba facing the mountain, seeing her distress and fear. You'd think—didn't the girl—why did she deny the power in herself? Deny it now in Ram's need when the two forces hung, evenly matched, with Ram's life balanced between?

He felt Tayba move uncertainly toward the cliff. Why was she so hesitant? He reached out, came into her mind to force her, to push his own call for Fawdref into her. She must be made to cry out to the wolves, to use the power of the bell in Ram's name. To command the wolves' greater strength. He paused, lifting his hand, then dropped it in his lap. She was so stubborn. And why did she stir him so? Why did a woman whose selfish desires ruled her, who could think of little but her own passions, stir him like this? Her selfish needs were the only urgency she knew; and yet her hidden, unwanted power was so fine. Was she going to let the stuff of her mind reach out now to help Ram, or was she going to stand there like a strictured ewe, staring stupidly at the damned mountain?

Ram lay dying, couldn't she. . . . Ram, whose mind could open like the sweeping winds; the boy would one day be a Seer without peer. Already he wove patterns so intricate even Jerthon had trouble following. Ram could not die, the child who had clung to Jerthon in terror when the Seer of Pelli tore at him, who lay balanced now on an abyss of such peril. Ram who had woven the images of wolves into the night air and made Venniver's guards

107

follow them. Jerthon looked across at Drudd, thinking angrily, *He* will *not die this night. He* will *not.*

But Drudd stared back at him coldly. "You should have slipped out of the tunnel and taken the bell yourself. She is not reliable."

"She will call Fawdref. She—Ram is her child. . . ."

"She doesn't care enough. She cares for Ram, but not for what he is. She does not care that to lose Ram would be to jeopardize—Ere itself. That means nothing to her, would not if you told her." Drudd scratched his bearded cheek irritably. "The damned girl is a danger. To you, to Ram, to us all. And she will defeat all we've worked for. You wait and see. The statue. . . ."

"We can't argue now, we haven't the strength for it. There is something in her, something—she has power, Drudd."

"She has a power better left alone. She doesn't want it. If you force her to it, we will all be sorry. There is betrayal in her. This plan—four years breaking our backs for it, and she could destroy it. She stinks of betrayal like a bad cheese."

Pol looked at Jerthon, his thin freckled face showing alarm; and Jerthon turned at once to the business at hand, felt the Seers of Pelli forcing in stronger, felt Ram's breathing falter. And Jerthon locked with HarThass in a straining hold of powers, weaving tangles of empty darkness to distract and confuse the Pellians, conjuring black holes in space beyond the Pellian's powers to balance. . . .

TAYBA CRAWLED up the cliff's side, crying out in fear and desperation to Fawdref. Her hands and legs were bleeding. She groped upward onto cliffs like black abysses above her, holding the bell, protecting it from harm. Her desperation for Ram was terrible. Fawdref *must* come. He must help. She could not command the bell. Would her desperate need be enough? And then suddenly she felt a force surrounding her, pressing upward with her as if she battled shoulder to shoulder with others. She felt her own strength and the strength of others as one, forcing back the darkness, shattering the desolation. She felt their power together—all of them—holding Ram, making Ram live; pushing the cold Seer back.

She stood on a summit calling out, commanding Fawdref now; and knew she was one with Jerthon and the Seers. She did not question; felt her own power rise in her in a surge that brought tears. . . .

And as she began to move upward again, clinging to stone, the boulders above her moved, and a bloodcurdling cry broke the night. Fawdref stood above her, his golden eyes on her. His voice terrible and powerful, his wild cry vibrating across the breadth of the night.

The pack was ranged around him on the cliff. Sentries stood out at either side. Fawdref started down the cliff toward her. He was an entity to himself, a ruler here; she was nothing. There was no gentleness in him now, as he had shown with Ram. She wanted to turn and run wildly and uselessly, was sick with fear as he moved cat-like down the cliff; felt his disdain for her. He looked at her coldly, with contempt.

She felt Jerthon urging her, supporting her. Fawdref paused on the ledge above her. Her hands shaking, she held up the bell, then knelt in the wolves' symbol of submission, the bell a talisman thrust up to him. She made a picture of Ram, of his fever and weakness; and she knew that Fawdref knew too well, saw all of it; she felt the wolf's heavy power as he battled with the dark forces alongside Jerthon, felt his cool command of her, felt again that sense of many forces poised in an intricacy of balance that she could not comprehend; knew that somehow she was the fulcrum on which they waited, that now she alone could tip that balance, in bringing the power of the bell close, in augmenting Fawdref's strength, in giving of that power in herself that she had so long denied. She clutched the bell in a cold grip, swung between terror and wonder. And suddenly Fawdref's howl filled the night, stunning her anew. The pack wolves echoed, their voices shaking the wind, opening a vast realm. She felt Ram reach out to her in desperate need. She felt something within her rise up in surging power, saw spaces open and tumble, break around her in terrifying vastness. She felt her own power come whole and strong at last. It terrified her. The wolves cried out, touching stars unborn and souls unmade in a powerful animal lament. In raw prayer they were linked, all of them, and infinity vibrated in the wolves' howling voices; infinity twisted inward into something larger than infinity, and she was part of it, she spoke beside Jerthon and Fawdref to command a vastness of space that left her breathless as they tore life from the cold realms of the dying to give it back to Ram.

And in the tumult, suddenly, Ram whispered.

His whisper stilled them like a shout. The wolves waited, heads lifted. Ram spoke fuzzily—then he shouted out in all his fury at the Pellian Seer, shouted with sudden, terrible strength.

She could feel the Pellian fall back, she could feel life fill Ram, feel the Seer turn away into blackness. In defeat.

She stood up, reached to touch Fawdref's muzzle. The wolf came down to press against her, nuzzle her. She laid her hand on the broad dome of his head. He looked up at her and grinned a fine wolf grin, amused and cruel. Very knowing. Then he turned away from her in one liquid movement and slipped up into the night. He vanished, the pack vanished; and she stood alone high on the black cliff.

Ram rose from his bed and stood looking toward the mountain, sobered after his close brush with death. He could not feel Fawdref with him now, could not feel Tayba, though he was filled with wonder at her sudden power unleashed, a power so long hidden. And he knew that already it was becoming a dream to her, that in a few minutes more she would have convinced herself it had never existed, that what she experienced had been Fawdref's doing, and Jerthon's.

He returned to his bed very tired and curled up to sleep, warm under the blankets that Skeelie drew over him.

The slaves ate a little of their cold meal, then slept too —all but Jerthon. He could not sleep, but lay in the dark cell thinking of Tayba. Why did she deny what she held within her? Selfish, Drudd was thinking drowsily. Jerthon closed his mind to Drudd. But it was true; if she admitted to such a power, then she must align herself either with good or with evil. And if that choice were for good rather than evil, she would not be able to pursue her own whims regardless of their consequences. Not when she could wield such power over others. A selfish, small view of the world she took, he thought with fury.

It was a waste to ignore such power as hers. It angered him. He felt Ram, half waking, probe in with childlike curiosity. *Why do you care? Why, Jerthon? Why do you care what Mamen does?*

It is a waste, Jerthon repeated. *Such power ignored is a waste.*

I see. Ram slept again, only puzzling a little at what Jerthon held back from him, an interest in Tayba that was not purely one of righteous anger.

Chapter Eight

ALONE ON THE CLIFF, Tayba stood looking down at the empty moon-washed plain, felt drained of all emotion and strength. No one spoke in her mind now. The power she had felt was gone—had never been there, was all illusion. Her aloneness stabbed at her like a knife. She started down the cliff trembling with apprehension and stood at last at the mountain's base, gripped with terror at the emptiness, at the looming boulders. The eerie expanse panicked her—and she began to run suddenly and wildly toward Burgdeeth, dodging boulders and the reaching shadows, shivering, until at last she could see the lights of the town.

And a figure was riding toward her.

Venniver. Venniver coming to find her; riding in a fury, beating his horse, his shoulders hunched, coming straight for her. She imagined his quick, fierce anger and stared around her uselessly for a place to hide, a shadow to conceal her. What would he say, finding her here? What would he think?

Maybe he won't be angry. Maybe . . . . She remembered the wolf bell beneath her tunic and pulled her cloak across it. She could tell him that she. . . . But he was on her, reining in his horse. She saw his face; fear sickened her. He swung down. She cringed away from him, tried to speak as he grabbed her arm. "Where in Urdd have you been! What are you doing out here!" His eyes were cold, appraising. "Who were you with? Who?"

"No one! I was with no one!"

"Don't lie to *me!*" He jerked her to him, twisting her. "I can break that arm if I choose. Now where is he?"

"I'm trying to tell you! There is no one!"

"You didn't come here alone! No one walks alone on this plain." He stared at her with disgust. "Who were you with! Where is he!"

"Who *would* I be with when I could be with you? Don't be stupid. Why would I . . . ." She sighed, reached out to him. "I was walking alone, Venniver. Ram is sick, I was upset. The moonlight—there is nothing out here. It seemed so peaceful—as if a prayer, here. . . ."

"A prayer! Great Urdd! Don't lie to me. You came here with some fracking guard!" He hit her full in the face, then spun her around to twist her arm behind her. "Some guard who—" His voice broke with fury. He slipped the stallion's reins over a boulder; the nervous animal plunged and reared. His fingers bit into her arm; he threw her down so her cloak and tunic ripped, terrifying her. Then he stopped suddenly, staring.

He straightened up, to back away from her.

The wolf bell lay beside her, touched by moonlight.

Tayba swallowed blood, felt the cut on her mouth. She watched him helplessly. Well, he couldn't know what the bell was. Why was he staring at it? Why would he. . . . He bent to pick it up almost as if it would burn him. He examined it, turned it over, held the clapper so it would not ring; looked for a long time with growing horror at the grinning bitch-wolf. Then he jerked her up, his fingers like steel, his voice shaking, nearly screaming. "What are you doing with *this*? I know what this is! I've heard the stories!" He stared at her, unbelieving. "You—you are one of *them!*" His voice dropped to a whisper. "You are a Seer. This—this is the bell of the wolf cult! You've been on the mountain with—*wolves!*"

He beat her then until she went limp under his hands, her mind sweeping blackness into the pain, confusing her. She felt herself dragged, then was forced to walk. She felt the stallion plunge against her where Venniver led him. She was forced on and on down the plain. Burgdeeth's lights swam before her. They were in the gardens, she thought; she could feel mawzee briars catch at her. She saw the back of the Hall but was not seeing properly, was so dizzy.

He forced her on. She was shivering, could hardly walk for the pain. She tried to pull her torn cloak around herself, wanted only to lie down. He stopped her at last. She saw the guard tower above the trees, heard the familiar ring of the iron door.

She was shoved into darkness, nearly fell, heard the door slam behind her.

She reached out and felt hands on her, felt the strength of someone supporting her. She hurt. Great Eresu she hurt.

SHE WOKE IN THE DIM, close cell. She tried to roll over, went sick with the pain that struck sharp through her arm and side. Her face felt swollen. She touched it hesitantly. Her exploring fingers brought pain along her left side, her left eye. Her lip was big and scabbed over. The candlelight was very dim, flickering. Little groups of slaves reclined on piles of hides, were turned away from her talking softly, paying no attention to her. Out of kindness? Or because they didn't care. She let her face drop down onto her arms. She would die in this place. She wanted to die.

"You will not die."

She lifted her face and turned until she could see Jerthon where he sat beside her. She saw that she lay on hides, was covered with a thick goathide.

"You will not die. But you do look somewhat battered. Here." He supported her head and held a mug for her. She drank greedily.

"More?"

She nodded, heard the water poured out, and drank again. "That is enough, you'll make yourself sick. Could you manage some bread?" Then, to her unspoken question, "Ram is all right. The fever is gone. The Seer has subsided into his black little hole—for the time being." He broke bread for her. "Your right arm works. Take the bread. Sit up now and try to eat a little."

Her ribs were very painful, were tightly bound. He helped her sit up. She leaned against the cell wall, nauseated with the effort. A few of the slaves looked at her, and a girl smiled. There was a warmth among them as they looked, a quiet solitude that reassured her. All but the stocky, short man there in the back. What made him

114

scowl so? That was the man called Drudd, the other forgeman.

The girl who had smiled was younger than the other four girls, little more than a child. Her hair shone like fire even in the dim light. Jerthon beckoned to her, and she came to sit beside Tayba. Jerthon said, "This is Derin. She will sleep beside you, in case there is anything you want in the night."

Derin said, "Dlos will bring herbs for the pain when she brings the morning meal. I put—I put what little we had in your water."

Tayba held out her hand. "Thank you. It does hurt." Suddenly she remembered the bell lying in the moonlight, remembered that Venniver had picked it up. She stared at Jerthon. "Does Venniver have it—the bell? What did he . . . ?"

"He has it. Ram—Ram wanted to charge into his rooms and take it. He's stubborn, that boy. It was all I could do to make him wait awhile." Jerthon searched Tayba's face, looked as if he would say more, then was silent.

She lay trying to puzzle it out, putting pieces together. *Why* had Ram been so ill? *Why?* What did Har-Thass . . . ? And suddenly it all did come together, the grotto, the Seer appearing on the high bridge; Ram's determined attitude afterward; the Seer's fury at Ram for something she did not before understand. She looked at Jerthon quietly. "You were in the grotto with Ram," she whispered. "You were there with him—just like tonight."

"Yes. We are five Seers here. We. . . ."

She laid her hand on his arm. "What—what did Ram See in the grotto? What was in that high cave that Har-Thass didn't want him to see, that he did see and came down so full of? He means—he made some commitment there." Her fingers tightened on Jerthon's arm, and she half rose to look at him, ignoring the pain. "What was it? What does Ram plan that—that HarThass would stop him from doing?"

Jerthon paused, studying her, sat for so long in silence she wondered if he would ever speak. When he spoke, it was reluctantly.

"Ram saw, in that cave—he saw pictures of a procession. He saw the gods lay to rest a box containing something of great power. Containing—the Runestone of Eresu. Ram—something is leading him, something compels him to bring that power out into Ere. There is need for it now. He is drawn there, and no one—not you, nor I—can stop him, now, from that quest."

"But he can't just . . . where will it lead him? Why must *he* go! He's only a child, he . . . Ram has the wolf bell. He has all the power anyone . . ."

He looked at her steadily. The others watched. The cell was very still. Drudd scowled. Derin took Tayba's hand in her small one. Jerthon said, "It is not for himself that he wants power. You don't think . . . it is a power that could help many, could change the lives of everyone in Ere for generations to come. Could stop what Venniver and those like him, what HarThass wants. Or could, in the hands of HarThass, bring havoc over Ere. It is so great a force. . . ." The light from the candle marked the clean lines of his face, the high Cherban cheekbones. She remembered her awe of him last night as the dark vastness twisted around her.

"If Ram does not seek that power, the Seer of Pelli will take it, now that he knows where it lies. He will climb Tala-charen for it. And if HarThass should hold that power. . . ." He took her hands. "I will show you what HarThass could do."

His grip was warm. He willed her to close her eyes. She fought him for a moment, then began to feel weightless. Her pain vanished. She drifted out of herself to move above Ere as if—as if she flew. She saw Ere stretching below her, saw rivers flowing out from the black peaks to find their way to the sea.

She saw small bands of men, primitive tribes with precarious holds on their little patches of land, saw warring Herebian bands killing them and driving them out. She saw the activity of hundreds of years, saw countries begin to form. She saw the volcanoes boil down across the land bringing terror and death, destroying all that men had built. Jerthon held her mind in his until she had seen the huge pageant of Ere's young history, seen Seers beheaded, seen them flee to the cities of the gods. She saw Seers ride out over Ere on the backs of the Horses of Eresu, filling men with hatred though they intended none of this. She saw evil Seers rise across the land to rule the little settlements, terrifying men into doing their bidding, and protecting men so they clung to them for leadership. Jerthon's eyes held her. He lifted her chin to look deep at her. He showed her the Herebian tribes raiding the nations; changes in borders and inner rule as powers struggled one against the other. She was seeing into the future now. She saw Carriol become a nation, and Burgdeeth as part of a new country. She saw that, as a river could split into many streams, Ere's future could take many ways. In one, the Pellian Seers ate up one country after another as HarThass and his successors, with the power of the Runestone of Eresu, enslaved peoples of Ere into one vast hierarchy of rule where men were as nothing.

In other streams of the future, men ruled themselves in a variety of activities, each as suited his own nature. The tangle of possible futures, of possible balances of power, dizzied her. And in all Ere's future, the Runestone was the key. And Ram, who vowed to bring that stone out of Tala-charen, was the one who held the balance now. On Ramad of Zandour lay the future of the countries of Ere.

"You," Jerthon said, beginning to pull her back from that infinite expanse, "you could not have seen all this, Tayba, were it not for the power you deny in yourself. When will you admit to it? When will you face the truth of yourself?" And she was too caught up in wonder to flare at him.

She woke from the vision quickly, was gripped by sudden pain from her wounds, watched Jerthon in silence as he drew her thoughts back from that terrible abyss of space and time. And one question burned in her mind. She groped at it, puzzled. If HarThass could change all of Ere's history with the Runestone, why had he waited so long to seek it? She looked at Jerthon deeply. "The Runestone must have been in Tala-charen for generations. Why . . . ?" And then, suddenly, she understood. "HarThass—HarThass didn't know before! He didn't See it until—until Ram went there to the grotto." She was twisting her hands; she scowled at them and put them in her lap. She could see by his face that she was right. "HarThass didn't see the Runestone until Ram—until he could see through Ram's mind that something was there! Until Ram had gone to the cave!"

"Yes," Jerthon said softly. "That is so."

"And if Ram—if he hadn't gone to the grotto. If he had never had the wolf bell, gone among the wolves, Har-Thass would have no idea. . . ."

"Yes, that is true. And if," Jerthon said softly, "if you had never lain with EnDwyl, Ram would not be here at all."

RAM WAS DRESSED in such a bundle of clothes, forced on him by Dlos, he thought he could not move. He tried to keep the lantern from clinking against stone as he crouched beneath Venniver's window, next to Skeelie. They could hear the men at supper, had seen Venniver quaffing ale at the long table as they slipped by. "I still say I'm the one to go in," Skeelie said, "you—"

"I want," Ram whispered as he pried the shutter loose, "I want to do it myself, Skeelie. Now be still—only, hiss if anyone comes." He climbed over the sill, took the lantern from her, lit it, and shone the light around, catching his breath at the grand furnishings, the rich colors. He went quickly to the chest at the foot of the bed.

He lifted the lid, found the key stuck down between side and bottom. He took the key to the fireplace, pushed away a strip of molding, found the lock. When Venniver's safe was open, he stared with wonder at the jewels there, the fine goblets and golden bowls. The wolf bell stood on the center shelf.

"Hurry!" Skeelie hissed. "Someone—hurry!"

He grabbed the bell, stuffed it in his tunic, replaced the key and was just over the sill when he heard voices. He dropped down on top of Skeelie, and they lay in a heap, not daring to move.

Two guards strode past, arguing. One said something about a donkey that made them stiffen. But the guards went on, unheeding, passing their donkey right by where he stood hobbled in the shadows.

They sorted themselves out, unhitched Pulyo, and hastened through shadow up toward the plain. They had already said good-bye to Dlos, were loaded with mawzee cakes and bread the old woman had slipped out of the sculler, with smoked meat and some chidrack eggs carefully wrapped. Skeelie led the donkey, taking a proprietary air with him after her sore trial getting him out of the herd. "He's mine now," she said, hugging the gray scruffy neck. "I stole him, and he's mine."

"Will Venniver come after us, do you think, if he finds we're gone?" Ram said.

"Why should he?"

"The donkey, for one thing. I still say, Skeelie. . . ."

"Would you want to carry all of the pack, blankets and food?"

"I still say we didn't need—"

"Yes we do. You don't know anything. Besides, Venniver won't come into the mountains. He's terrified of them."

They heard the wolves, then.

The wolves had begun to come out of the caves, crying out at the night, showing themselves for an instant then slipping away down the mountain toward the children, their eyes like ice as they paced and stared down across the shadows. Ram heard their cries and thrilled to them, remembering Gredillon's words, read so long ago from an ancient book she had kept wrapped in silk in her cupboard.

For NiMarn shaped a bell of bronze that would call the wolves out of the wild night or send them cringing down among the shallow rock-caves where they denned; a magic of power concentrated in the metal and the fashioning. He stared up the mountain, heard Fawdref's wild call, and quickened his pace up the plain, the little donkey trotting along as if he went everyday to join wolves.

In the morning the slaves were taken out to work, and Tayba left alone in the cell. A guard, herding the others out, said, "You will be given a few days to mend. But

119

hurry up about it, Venniver does not like to feed idlers. You will be expected to work like the rest." When they all had gone, she felt the darkness of the cell close in around her, her wrists prickling oddly at the thought that she was locked in, trapped here like some wild thing caught in a furrier's cage.

She lay huddled in the cell ignoring the bread and water Derin had left her, the herbs Dlos had brought. She tried to remember all that Jerthon had shown her and could not. Some of it, yes. But a haziness came over the pictures, maddening her. There was something else, though. Something that lingered in her mind, secret and urgent. Had she gotten the thought from Jerthon? It was as if there was something they would not trust her with, something they had shielded from her.

But she did know. She knew. She rose so quickly the pain brought tears and began to prowl the cell. What was it that Jerthon had hidden in his thoughts, did not want her to know? How could she know something he had not intended her to see? Unless she. . . .

"No! I do not have that power!" She stood staring down at the pile of hides where Jerthon had slept, trying to shake off the unwanted knowledge. And she knew, with perfect clarity, that if she pushed those hides away—she thrust the hides back with her foot and saw the loose, unmortared stones underneath. She knelt, folded the hides back, and began to lift out the stones.

Beneath them was a wide plank. She lifted it out, and knelt there staring down into a black pit.

Crude steps went down, to disappear in darkness. Three lanterns stood on the top step; she reached for one, and struck flint, adjusted the wick. Now she could see the bottom step, and the beginning of a tunnel. She started down, then turned back, leaving the lantern on the stairs.

She covered the loose stones with hides, then pulled hides over the plank and pulled that over the hole behind her as she descended.

The tunnel ran on farther than her light reached. Heavy timbers supported the roof—Venniver's timbers, she thought, grinning. And Venniver's stones and dragon bone mortared into the walls.

She had gone some distance when she came to a pile of loose dirt where the slaves must recently have been digging. A side tunnel opened here, smaller and unmortared. A stack of long timbers stood at the mouth. She counted twenty exactly and could hear Venniver shouting, *Where in Urdd do timbers go! Where does someone hide timbers! You don't. . . .* She went on, smiling to herself.

Soon her way was blocked by the tunnel's end. Shovels had been left here, a pick, an adz. A sled for carrying dirt. There was everything here. How in Urdd had they gotten it all, right out from under Venniver's nose?

"Skeelie stole it," Jerthon said quietly. She spun at his voice, her lantern careening light up the walls.

"Skeelie is clever and quick. She could steal Venniver's beard off his face." He came toward her. His clear green eyes held her. "I wish I could—could be sure of you." He made a barrier between them that she could not broach. "Well, what you have already seen is enough to get us all killed." He took her lantern from her and held it up; and where the tunnel had stopped in a fall of dirt, now it was suddenly open in an illusion so real and sudden she gasped. It went further than the light could reach. "That is how it will be," Jerthon said. "We. . . ." he stopped speaking, startled, as two figures appeared there ahead, young girls, their hair long down their backs. This was not a vision Jerthon was giving her, this had come unbidden. She could feel his sharp interest as the brown-haired girl began to rummage in a crevice in the tunnel wall; Jerthon caught his breath as the girl drew her hand from the niche, closed around something small and glowing; and suddenly the tunnel began to grow light, to open out, the space becoming huge and so brilliant Tayba could hardly look.

An immense space opened out before them and seemed to be expanding. There were vague mountains in the distance; but the towering winged figures close at hand made her go weak with awe, want to kneel. Their human torsos rose above the horselike bodies, tall, burnished; and their wings flashed against the brilliance of expanding light. Their eyes, their faces held wonders that made her want to cry out, drowned her in a world quite beyond her.

121

You are come, they cried, and their voices held a terrible joy. *You must reach out, you will reach out—if you are the chosen.* She was clutching Jerthon's hand.

The vision vanished. There was blackness. Tayba had heard something drop to the floor, saw dimly that one of the girls knelt to search across the dirt for it—then that, too, vanished. She stood staring, felt Jerthon beside her, looking up to see him as stricken as she.

He shook free of the vision at last. "I have to go back. I will be missed." He seemed not to want to speak of what he had seen, to lock it privately within. He led her back along the tunnel, then turned away from her into the side tunnel. "This goes into the pit." He smiled for the first time, then swung away, brushing the wall with his shoulder. Loose grains of dirt fell, then dirt fell from the roof—she didn't know what was happening, she was covered by falling dirt; she couldn't see, felt Jerthon grab her shoulder and push her roughly away—Jerthon was there in falling dirt, she saw a timber fall. Dirt roared down, she dove under the timber reaching for Jerthon, jammed her shoulder under it so it nearly knocked her flat, the pain making her cry out.

She sprawled beneath the timber's weight covered with dirt, and could feel Jerthon buried beneath her.

She twisted over, clawing at the dirt beneath her. *Jerthon!* His face was covered, he could not breathe. She fought dirt, twisted down into an impossible position, digging, scraping dirt with her hands. The pain in her side tore at her. She felt Jerthon try to move his leg, felt his panic. She clawed like an animal, and at last could feel his shoulder, his neck, began to dig dirt away from his face; could feel his mouth at last, felt him suck in breath. The pain in her side was like knives. She clawed dirt away from his mouth, his nose. She could feel his breath on her hand. Nausea swept her. She began to clear dirt from his eyes, could feel dirt falling on her back.

Something touched her back, she started violently, then realized someone was clearing dirt from her body. She twisted around and saw Drudd pushing a block of wood in next to her to support the timber. He wedged another block in farther down, then began digging with a small

122

spade as she held her hands to protect Jerthon's face. Drudd cleared her first, to get at Jerthon, then she dug beside him. Jerthon kept himself quiet with great effort, she thought. He was sweating, his jaws clenched. She thought he wanted to fight the confining dirt mindlessly, as she would have.

When he was free at last, he stood in the tunnel looking at them, very white, collecting himself. There was nothing for anyone to say. Drudd and Jerthon soon went around the slide and back up to the pit.

Shaken, Tayba returned to the cell and began replacing the plank and stones. When she had finished, she sat down on the skins wishing the nausea would pass, wishing her hands would stop trembling.

What had caused the cave-in? Had it been a natural thing, there where the tunnel was yet unsupported? Or had the Pellian Seer brought it down on Jerthon in a moment of cruel retribution for Jerthon's part in saving Ram? Meant, she thought, shivering, to kill both of them there?

She did not know. Perhaps neither did Jerthon. Perhaps he had been too terrified to wonder or to care.

And when she thought of Jerthon's knowledge of her, of the power within her that she would give anything to be rid of, she wondered if, were it to happen again, she would be quite so quick to gamble her life to save someone who not only knew of that power, but expected her to come to terms with it in a way she could not bear to do.

Part Three

Part Three

The Stone

Chapter Nine

THE SEER OF PELLI turned from the window to stare at EnDwyl. Below him along the bay, where a handful of wharves fanned out, the boats were bringing in a catch of sherpin. Farther down, some farm wagons had set up to trade grain and vegetables, ignoring the more conventional vender's stalls. He was scowling. His faded red beard, cut into two points in the style of the Pellian Seers, made him look like a goat. His eyes, blue when he was young, were nearly colorless. He threw his cape over a chair as he spoke.

"It does not pay, my dear EnDwyl, to be too certain. You do not understand the skills—or the limits—of Seers. You think we can do more than we are able."

"Common Seers have limits, perhaps. But you are the Seer of Pelli." EnDwyl, having come directly from the sea baths, seemed the cooler of the two, his yellow hair brushed smooth and his white tunic immaculate. "Pellian Seers are not limited, surely. The descendants of the wolf cult—"

"We, my dear EnDwyl, are not descendents of the wolf cult. That is the problem. Urdd knows, if we were we'd not have to go to all this flaming trouble for the boy and his cursed bell."

"Cursed? You'd give the entire fortune of Pelli for the blasted bell—and for the boy. What kind of business is that for the ruler of Pelli, all this fuss over a toy to turn wolves into pets."

"Not pets, EnDwyl. Do you forget the wolves that greeted you outside Burgdeeth? *Accomplices, EnDwyl! Powerful accomplices!* Do you forget the forces the boy and wolves called forth, the skill with which they battled us? And you," he added, "you are the descendant of the bell. You should have some feeling for it, even if the blood in you is latent. It is your blood that created Ramad —yours, and the Seer's blood in your—in Tayba. That boy—that boy holds a power out of the ancient past that even I do not fully understand. The bell has only served to focus his force. And the boy's power, and the power of the bell are powers I mean to control. Though if we do not wrest it from the pup soon, he will command a far greater power. And I will not have that, EnDwyl! The stone on Tala-charen is a force that boy must never possess."

EnDwyl said insolently, "You have tried to subdue the boy and failed. And there are these slaves—they shield their plans too well, HarThass. You don't know—"

"I know their plans. I could easily use those plans against them, if it weren't for that boy scrambling up Tala-charen. But if the boy reaches Tala-charen's peak first, and so controls the stone. . . ."

"And so we ride to Burgdeeth," EnDwyl said irritably. "With twelve fighting men to battle Jerthon and the slaves while the Pellian Seers use their forces on the boy. *I* don't think—"

"You don't think, EnDwyl. That is your problem. Do you have a better plan? Are you more skilled than Seers? Can you bring the horrors of those mountains against Ramad as I can?"

"Do you really believe, HarThass, that even without the stone's power against you, you can defeat the boy and Jerthon and that lot. I—"

HarThass's gaze burned into him. "Yes EnDwyl? You what?"

EnDwyl swallowed. "I don't know. I—maybe the slaves' power even without the stone is too great. And now—and now, with this thing you say is awakened in Tayba. . . ."

HarThass selected a cicaba fruit from the silver tray beside him. "That hasn't lasted. Already the girl has nearly hidden it from herself. She is terrified of having such power. She may. . . ." He smiled coldly. "She may help us more than you can imagine. She is afraid of this power of hers, she is afraid of Jerthon because he sees

it. If we can turn her against him—she has the fine instincts of a traitor. Jerthon represents a challenge to her
she cannot bear to face. She might well be persuaded to
destroy that challenge under certain circumstances."

"But Venniver has treated her shabbily, maybe she
won't. . . ."

"She likes his treatment, don't you see that? She will
come crawling back to him with very little encourage-
ment." He turned away, then turned back to stare at
EnDwyl. "You leave the girl to me. And you, EnDwyl—
you be ready to ride as soon as those cursed soldiers get
here with the mounts from Sangur. Why you let them—"

"They are better horses. You traded for them yourself. How was I to know. . . ."

"You could have sent down for them a month ago.
Well." HarThass raised an eyebrow. "I don't suppose you
relish riding back into that plains country, EnDwyl." He
stared pointedly at the jagged scar across EnDwyl's jaw,
and the mass of welts that crippled his legs. "I don't suppose you relish meeting wolves again."

EnDwyl's hand was drawn to his cheek, but he did
not respond to HarThass's rudeness. "I don't understand
why the slaves wait. Why did they not leave Burgdeeth
as soon as they had that tunnel open? What keeps the
fools there? If they want to capture and rule Burgdeeth
as you say, they would not even need a tunnel. If their
power is so great, they have simply to warp Venniver's
thoughts until he sets them free and gives them the cursed
town."

"There is something in Venniver that makes his mind
unreliable. He can be moved for a few moments, then
he is impervious to most skills. You cannot keep him
controlled, you can only direct him on occasion. Some
latent Seer's blood, like you, EnDwyl.

"But beyond that, those Seers are an odd lot. They
remain quite willingly, with some wild idea about com-
pleting the tunnel." HarThass snorted. "Something to do
with visions of the future. What rubbish. The future is to
be manipulated regardless of visions—to be bent to the
strongest will in spite of all the wild visions you can name.
This Jerthon and his slaves are dreamers, they have no

real sense of value. Visions! They only show you what might be, not what will!

"At any rate, we will have Burgdeeth for ourselves soon enough.

"But I tell you this, EnDwyl. I will not allow that boy to scale Tala-charen. *I* will ride up Tala-charen to retrieve that stone!" He smiled. "How fortunate that the boy discovered where it lay. Once we have the stone," he said lightly, "once we have subjugated Burgdeeth, that town will become our first outpost. From it we can work southward at our leisure. We will ease Zandour and Aybil and Farr into positions that will destroy them so slowly they will never know they have been taken. We will use Venniver's own plan, his books, the religion he has invented, his statute—and we will use the stone. No one will resist that combination. But we will do it slowly. I like to do things slowly and see men twist in the coils of the stricturing I put on them." He leaned back, crossing his legs and flicking some lint from his sandals.

"Is that why you did not march into Burgdeeth long ago? Because you want to do it slowly?" EnDwyl asked sarcastically. "Not because you failed in manipulating the boy into coming to you willingly, HarThass?"

"You had best watch your tongue, EnDwyl. I didn't see you and that cursed Seer who died on the plain having any great success with the boy—or with the wolves he commands." HarThass smiled and leaned back. "Well, the wolves will soon be ours. And I like the idea of the boy walking before us down Tala-charen with his wrists bound and those wolves grovelling around him. We will walk with wolves then, EnDwyl. And we will use their powers at our pleasure.

"But that boy won't be easy to—"

"When I finish with the boy, he will have no choice in the matter."

No TRAIL WAS VISIBLE SAVE, sometimes, a vague cupping or turning that might mark an ancient path. Ram traveled by instinct, by the pull of power that so beckoned to him, and by Fawdref's sure guidance. They crossed meadows where dead sablevine was frozen into ice and the ice itself torn up and tumbled as if something huge had spent its fury here, ripping with claws like knives at the frozen ground. They were cold, always cold. The wraps Dlos had so stubbornly bundled them into were never quite enough to keep out the freezing wind. They climbed between monster shapes of twisted black stone, between clusters of columns like headless trees, formed by some wild excess of the volcanoes. They passed deep through narrow sunless canyons flanked with walls like black glass, so smooth they could see themselves. "We look," Skeelie said, bending and dancing about so her reflection was thick then thin and long, "like—like the souls of the dead."

Ram bent to hug Fawdref, who had turned away from his own reflection in disgust. The wolves seemed to find no humor in their distorted images. "Old dog! Can't you laugh at yourself?"

Fawdref touched Ram's cheek with his muzzle, then looked again into the deep black mirror. He was, he let Ram understand, considering that.

As they rose higher up the mountain, the power of something dark increased, watching them relentlessly. Yet it never showed itself; if indeed it had any form to show. Late the second afternoon the wolves killed a buck, and they stopped early to roast the haunch. It was difficult to find firewood this high on the mountain, but the droppings of wild goat and stag made a hot blaze. The children lay back against the packs, smelling the roasting meat, watching the wolves gorge on the carcass and little Pulyo grazing beyond them. Pulyo raised his head once, laid his ears back and snorted, rolling his eyes so the whites showed. At once the wolves were alert, staring up toward a mass of black stone.

"Did it move?" Skeelie said. "Did the stone move?"

"I—I don't know."

They watched for a long time, but nothing moved. The animals settled down to feed; but Fawdref's message was plain in Ram's mind. An evil was there, stirred from sleep by the Pellian Seer. Not yet fully alive, but malevolent and very able to breathe life into itself when it chose.

131

Ram felt the forces building around them. And the very sweep of opposing forces seemed to be pulling a curtain aside, through which another realm of existence could be glimpsed. That realm, to which his spirit had always yearned blindly, was so immense that its very size made it invisible, as a gnat would view a great, fierce animal and be unable to comprehend what it was. This journey, these forces building, were as a key to that other world, which in time would show itself to all men.

All around them the forces converged, the Pellian's evil preparations, Jerthon's long plan coming to its crux, Venniver's stubborn self-interest—Tayba's precarious balance between self and something more than self. The power of good on Tala-charen, and the powers of all the evil of Ere, seeking. . . .

JERTHON AND DRUDD supported the bronze wing between them over the coals, heating the edge to be braised. Sweat ran down their faces, and little black gnats buzzed maddeningly. Jerthon looked up occasionally to watch the line of slaves carrying the cast pieces up from the pit. Derin appeared, bent nearly double under the weight of a bronze head, and Tayba struggled up behind, supporting the neck. Girls bent like work animals, their hair plastered with sweat.

The forge fire flared up. He rearranged the coals. This new fire, laid in the square, caught the wind and displeased him. He turned to adjust the metal baskets filled with coals that hung along the body of the Horse of Eresu, where the wing would be attached. The horse stood hollow and alone, headless, wingless, secured to the base; and the hollow base was set deep into dragon bone, ready to open itself secretly to the tunnel. He watched Tayba climb back down the pit, her dark tangled hair falling over her face, and felt her tiredness as if it were his own. Drudd said, "Does it please you that the women work like donkeys?"

"It can't be helped."

"It could if we were long gone from this place."

"Keep your voice down. They would be working just as hard, clearing land."

"But what is it all for!" Drudd whispered, scowling. "The future can change. You've no—visions show only what might be. To stay here, building this statue, when—"

"A vision of the future can change. But five visions? Or five different times?" Jerthon looked at Drudd across the edge of the wing. "And more important, in all times—if we do not succeed in taking Burgdeeth and stopping Venniver—the statue will be needed. You know as well as I that those few who question Venniver's teachings will need something to tell them that there is another way. Do you think . . . a way of truth, Drudd! They will not know, those children born and isolated here, that there is a way of freedom. They will think their own instincts are evil just as Venniver teaches them. Unless—unless they can see something that tells them differently. Something that excites their true instincts, makes them yearn. . . ."

"But won't Venniver realize? . . ."

"Venniver sees what he wants to see. He sees a statue denoting power, a statue that will put the seal of truth on his teachings, will help to subject men. He will see no more than that."

"So you build a symbol," Drudd said. "And he means to kill you when it's finished."

"We will be out and beheading his guards when he comes to kill me." Jerthon turned away, and when he looked back Venniver was entering the square, came at once to stand beside the statue, appraising it silently.

Then he turned to watch Tayba struggle up over the rim of the pit with the end of a cast wing. Jerthon tried to probe his mind, but the man could not be touched. Seer's blood. Yet the man had no skills, only this mindless blocking as if by instinct.

Well he hadn't blocked enough to hide the wolf bell; Ram had winnowed into his thoughts as cleverly as a mouse in the mawzee, seen and stolen the bell and Venniver did not even know it was gone—yet.

When he found it gone, though, his rage would bring bellows that ought to be heard clear in Sangur. Jerthon hid a smile.

At least Venniver couldn't blame Tayba. She hadn't

133

been near his fancy room in some while. Jerthon watched the man step toward her, then stiffened as he jerked her up from where she had knelt to set down her burden. She lost her balance, the bronze wing tipped, throwing its weight on Derin, and the child fell beneath the wing.

Jerthon moved to help her, but Drudd held his arm in a steel grip. They watched as Saffoni stepped out of line to lift the wing, her dark hair hiding her expression. Derin rolled free and seemed unhurt.

Venniver had paid no attention to Derin; she was nothing. He stood gripping Tayba's shoulder. She stared back at him with hatred, her color rising, her fists clenched. But there was something more than fury in her eyes. Jerthon watched her with cold apprehension.

"Look at yourself, my fine Tayba! Look at your matted hair and your dirty face. You look—you're no better than an animal!" He pushed her toward a guard. "Take her and have the old women bathe and dress her, then bring her to my rooms." He turned away, dismissing them both. The guard wrenched Tayba around, grinning at his fellows, then marched her off through the square accompanied by the guards' rude catcalls. Jerthon held his fury with great effort and turned once more to the brazing.

RAM BUILT up the fire. The goat dung was growing short, but he dared not let the blaze die. The wolves paced endlessly, staring out at the night. Pulyo brayed, and Skeelie pulled him farther back among the boulders and hushed him. The mountain at their back felt solid and protective.

After supper they had moved on, climbing up into a land of enormous upheaval, great cliffs of stone ripped away and lying tilted. As the evening light had faded, the climb grew colder, and they had begun to see flows of ice cutting away between the stone. They had made camp and the small fire in a cupped place against the mountain, sat watching the tilted cliffs of stone lighten as the moon rose. Suddenly the wolves growled, and Skeelie paused with her hand half lifted, staring.

There, where moonlight touched a thick bed of ice,

134

something moved within the ice. An immense shape, trapped in the frozen mountain of white. The children looked and could not move, saw its eyes behind the ice. It faded, the ice seemed to ripple; then it reappeared closer to them. Skeelie said, "The fire—will the fire keep it away?"

"Maybe," Ram said doubtfully. He looked at the pitiful fire, fed with dung. "Maybe," he said again, and knelt, held the wolf bell over the flame so the flicking light caressed the rearing bitch-wolf—and slowly he began to draw the fire out, to take it into himself and into the bell, to make it a part of the bell's power.

The wolves moved beyond the firelight toward the ice. Ram made the fire rise to run along his fingers, his arms, in a wild blaze.

The ice cracked sharply as the creature began to push up through it. Ram made fire leap and blaze out of his hands. The white monster slid up out of the ice. It was huge, weasel-like, big as seven horses. Ram cast fire up at it, gave fire to the wolves so they were flaming death-wolves. Together they stalked the creature as it slid down toward them, its belly slipping over the ice and down onto stone, its eyes never leaving them as it sought the warmth of living blood. The wolves were flaming giants raging toward the slinking weasel. It reared, hissing, its icy tail lashing, its huge pale eyes gleaming—and the flame washed over it so it cried out its rage in a shrill scream. Fire tore at it, burning, melting.

Wolves leaped, blazing. Ram threw fire on it, was a human tower of fire.

At last, defeated, the ice-weasel slunk away. Ram could smell its burning flesh. It shrank, twisted, down into the ice. Ram stood high on the ice watching it disappear and could feel HarThass's black rage. The ice drew together. The wolves' teeth shone white against their lolling tongues.

Ram returned soberly to the fire and sat staring into it with wonder at what he had wrought—and with the lonely cloak of fear wrapping him. For he had felt Har-Thass like a dark incubus choking away his power so it

135

had taken all his strength to bring the fire. Could he, as they drew closer to Tala-charen, continue to hold against the dark Seer? Yet beneath that straining effort, beneath the limits he had fought to extend, lay a power still greater in himself, untapped and dormant; a power he had not yet learned to reach. A power he must reach.

TAYBA WAS LOCKED into Venniver's rooms and left to herself. She had been bathed and dressed, like a child. Old Semma and Poncie had found the whole episode very amusing. Her temper raged. She stood looking at the fine room wondering what to destroy first. She was well bruised. She'd left scratches on the guard's face deep enough to kill the man if they festered, and she hoped they would. She stood staring at the cold fireplace, then knelt and laid a fire from the wood in the basket. She wasn't going to sit in a cold room shivering. She crouched there warming herself, trying to decide what to do. She hated Venniver. She thought she would kill him. What did he have in mind, bringing her here? She sat looking around the room, letting its luxury touch her in spite of her anger.

She didn't want to go back to that cell. She didn't want to have to face Jerthon's assessments of her, which had become so very painful. Maybe. . . .

She looked up as the lock turned.

Venniver entered and stood looking down at her. She stayed where she was, crouching, warming herself, undignified and not caring. To Urdd with him. His hard eyes made her swallow. She stared up at him coldly. His voice was measured. "Now that you are clean . . ." He moved toward her. "We will talk. Where did you get the bell? We will start with that."

"You could have asked me that when you found it instead of beating me. I would have told you; there was nothing about it to hide. I found it on that cursed mountain, in a cave, and I wish I never had."

"You said you weren't on the mountain. You said you were walking in the moonlight."

"I didn't say I wasn't on the mountain. You didn't give

me a chance to tell you anything. I had been on the mountain. I'd walked all night, praying for Ram. Out there—near the gods—"

"I don't want your lies! Tell me where you got the bell!"

"I am telling you where. In a cave. I thought it was— what is it? Why do you go on about it? What is so important about it?"

He stared at her for a long time. She looked back defiantly, her heart pounding. At last he said, "We will go up on the plain. You will call the wolves, my fine Tayba. You will use that bell. If the wolves come to you and do not kill us, then I will know that you lie. If they attack us, then. . . ." He smiled. "Then I will know you speak truly." He took up his sectbow and knife. "Get up."

She looked at him coldly, but afraid. He was quite mad. Well, the wolves were not on the mountain, could not be called. They were all with Ram. And didn't he know the bell was gone? She stared at him with rising fear. "If I could bid wolves—if I had such power as that, you would never have locked me in that cell. Did you think of that? If I were a Seer, you would never have found me on the plain, Venniver."

"You will bid the wolves come down. You will bid them lie down before me—"

"I cannot! Don't you understand! I know nothing of such things. What makes you believe anyone could call wolves?"

He turned to the chest at the foot of the bed, opened it, removed the key, then fit that to the lock beside the fireplace. She watched him, terrified.

He opened the safe, reached—and stared, his hand poised. Then at last he swung to face her. *"You have taken it!"* His shout filled the room. *"The bell is gone— you. . . ."*

She stared at him dumbly when he hit her, went limp under his hands.

"Where is it?"

"I don't have it. I don't understand. . . ."

137

He pulled her up and marched her to the window, unlocked the shutters, threw them back and forced her to climb through. He prodded her with his sectbow, then when she resisted, drew his knife to force her on. The wind was bitter cold, whipped the thin dress around her. The moons were pale slivers, the stars small and icy. They walked until Burgdeeth's lights lay well behind them; he prodded her cruelly when she turned to look. When they stood between twisting stone giants, where even Burgdeeth's lights were not visible, he stopped, halting her with a rude hand on her arm, pulling her around to stare down at her, his face grim and determined. "Call the wolves. You need no bell—if you have the skill." And when she cringed from him, "You will call the wolves down. Or you will die here."

She tried to think what to do. His knife flicked close to her face. "You have the knowledge of Seers. Call them. Bring them down to me."

"I cannot, Venniver. I told you."

"The bell comes from Zandour. You brought it here. Why else would. . . ." His voice died as he stared past her. She turned slowly to look.

Wolves were there. Dark slinking wolves coming in between the boulders, beginning to circle them, their heads lowered, their eyes cold; they made no sound, must have watched in hidden silence as Venniver forced her up the plain. She tried to contain her panic, looked for Fawdref among them, for pale Rhymannie—and then real terror swept her.

This was not Fawdref's band. These thin, creeping animals were not his wolves. They were smaller, their eyes not the knowing eyes of the wolves she knew, but the cold eyes of hunters moving intently forward to the kill.

She spun on Venniver. "Draw your bow. Shoot them. They'll kill us, Venniver!" She wanted to run, knew they would leap at once. "Kill them before they kill us!" The circle drew in, complete. Their eyes never looked into her eyes, but shifted, appraising each movement. Now she felt Venniver's fear, saw his sudden realization. "You can't. . . ." He raised his bow. His look was incredulous. "But you are a Seer—you. . . ."

"Kill them!" She jerked his knife from its sheath and turned to face the snarling band as a wolf leaped. She spun and plunged her knife in; its teeth caught her arm. She struck again and again in terror, its weight on her, trying to keep her balance—it fell at last as others leaped. She heard the bowstring sing, saw a wolf twist and fall, another. A wolf lunged against her shoulder nearly toppling her, its teeth at her throat. She stabbed and stabbed into the soft stomach as she fell, felt the animal go limp on top of her, heard the bow snap, saw wolves tearing at Venniver, dragging at him. She was torn and bleeding, dizzy. She thought the wolves had backed away. She felt Venniver beside her, trying to pull her up.

Seven wolves lay dead. The others were going away as if—as if they had been called, were slinking away up the dark plain. Venniver was holding her, pressing something to her throat trying to stop the blood. She shivered as he lifted her.

THE POWERS THAT STAYED the wolves pulled back and separated, hung poised for moments as one assessed the other; then all three turned away. Skeelie watched Ram, but could make little of what had happened. "Why did the Seer of Pelli help you? Why would he . . .? And help Jerthon? Why would he care if Tayba died or Venniver either?"

"Sometimes I wish you were a boy and didn't talk so much."

"I only. . . ." She looked back, saw the dark shadows beneath his eyes. "I'm sorry. I don't understand, that's all."

"HarThass—HarThass thinks to *use* Mamen—against Jerthon," he said sickly. "And he needs Venniver. If Venniver dies, Jerthon will take Burgdeeth at once."

"But why would Jerthon help her then, if Venniver would use her against him?"

"I think Jerthon—that Jerthon is a fool sometimes. Go to sleep, Skeelie! It's the middle of the night!" He threw

139

some goat dung on the fire and snuggled closer to Fawdref. The dark wolf sighed in his sleep. "Old dog! You
never even woke. I never even needed you!"

Fawdref opened one eye and pushed his nose into
Ram's shoulder.

And in Pelli, HarThass paced, puzzling over how easily his powers had blended with those of Jerthon and
Ram. Puzzling how to turn this to his advantage.

He saw Tayba's fear and pain then and stopped pacing
to touch her mind, very vulnerable now, to weave a spell
that soothed her, took away her dark thoughts—that
warmed her toward him, destroyed suspicion. . . .

In the slave cell Jerthon paced too, disturbing everyone. Well, his thoughts alone would have disturbed them.
He was not thinking of HarThass or of Ram. He saw
the Pellian soothe Tayba, then saw Venniver bandage
her and cover her. He felt his pulse quicken in anger
and was disgusted with himself.

He rose at last, wound tight as a spring, and jerked
the hides away from the tunnel opening, lit a lantern
and went down to where they had been setting new sup-
ports. He stood beneath the last timber and reached to
touch the place where they would soon cut through into
the statue's base. Then he turned back to the niche he
had carved into the tunnel wall, stood remembering the
vision he and Tayba had seen here, the gods, the brown-
haired girl bending to retrieve something. . . .

Had he carved the niche because of the vision? But
he had not; had always intended to put it there to hold
the small relics Derin had collected: a basket of pot-
shards, pieces of jewelry, a locket, three gold belt links,
all found as they dug stone near the grove. It was as if
the grove itself had been linked to the sacred city and to
that time when Seers lived freely here. The relics themselves brought vibrations, brought visions of splendor and
peace that stirred them; they would be left in this place
for others, for slaves who might come after them and
need such gentle reminders of a better time. He felt
Drudd behind him, was annoyed that Drudd had followed him down.

He turned, looked at Drudd a moment in anger, then

went to sit beside him on a pile of stone. Drudd said, "You watched Venniver make up with her. You torture yourself watching them."

"She—there is a goodness in her, a strength in her. HarThass would destroy that. I want—I want the power in her to come right."

"You lust after her. Be honest."

"That too, I suppose."

"HarThass would use her to kill you. Can't you see it, man! Have you taken leave of all your senses?"

"He will use her only if she lets him." He looked at Drudd unhappily. "Don't you think I know what she is? But beneath that—there is something more. I don't mean to let HarThass destroy it."

Drudd turned away muttering.

So he sat there deliberately watching Venniver and Tayba, forcing his mind to hold them, letting all of it twist inside him, saw and heard them so clearly he could have been standing in Venniver's ornate rooms, before the fire Venniver had just knelt to light.

Venniver had pulled a chair up beside the bed. Jerthon had a terrible desire to sit in it, to make himself *be* there, make her know he was there. Instead he watched Venniver return to it and put his arms around Tayba. She woke from a light doze and lay looking at him quietly. "You really didn't know," Venniver said, "what the bell was. What it could do."

"How could I have known?"

"Once," he said, "I went up the mountains and into the ancient caves. The wolves came out from everywhere, were there suddenly all around me. I turned and walked away from them, and they followed me down the mountain. They never touched me, they just walked behind me—looking."

Jerthon could feel her effort to understand him.

"They looked at me the way a man would. I—I wanted those wolves. I wanted them! Can you understand that? Once—once wolves like that were slaves to men. I wanted that, Tayba. And—and tonight, I wanted you to give me that."

141

Jerthon sickened, feeling her response. She understood Venniver exactly. She was not repelled by his lust, quite the opposite. She drew him to her and kissed him. Jerthon turned his mind away in disgust. Maybe Drudd was right. And yet—and yet he could not let that other part of her go.

Chapter Ten

THE WAY GREW too narrow and steep for the donkey. Skeelie had her arms around his shaggy neck, trying to hide tears. "We can't just leave him, Ram. He'll starve. Or something will kill him here."

"You should have thought of that."

"I did, but I thought—well, that there would be a valley somewhere with grass and water, and he'd stay. But there's nothing here, only stone. And now—now we've seen the other wolves, the common wolves that would kill him—oh, he's been a good donkey, Ram. Couldn't you—couldn't you lay a spell on his mind? Make him go home again, and quickly?

"I can try," Ram said uncertainly. He rubbed the donkey's nose and fondled it in the way it liked. Then, slowly and warmly, he let his mind flow into Pulyo's as if they were one. As if they shared all memory, all feeling. He thought of the trail back, and of Burgdeeth, warm and safe. He thought of Pulyo going back hastily, cautiously, along that wild trail.

At last Pulyo raised his head, put forward his ears, stared back down the trail, and began to bray.

Ram loosed him and patted his rump. The little animal set off at a trot, soon had broken into a gallop. As he rounded the first bend of the narrow path, his braying echoed back and forth between the peaks. Skeelie said, "I hope he gets *that* out of his system. He'll have every wolf in twenty miles following."

Ram thought of silence, stealthy silence. The idea might be foreign to a donkey, but the braying stopped at last. "Go in safety," Ram whispered.

They moved up along precipices now. And then at the edge of a sheer drop, the ground cracked suddenly beneath Ram's feet; Skeelie grabbed him, Fawdref lurched, pressing him back. They stood pushing against the wall of stone behind them, Skeelie very white, Fawdref unwilling to move away from Ram. The wolf's warmth, so close, was comforting. Ram looked at the broken precipice, and down to the mile-deep valley into which he would have fallen. Into which the rock had fallen clattering, then, without sound. They had not heard it hit. He picked up a stone, meaning to drop it down, but the thought sickened him. Skeelie said, "I thought the ground moved—before the cliff broke." She was chilled into silence. They stared at the edge where stones had sheered away as cleanly as if they had been hit by an ax. And Fawdref looked at Ram with pain. Ram knew he felt the agony of not having foreseen that falling stone.

The near accident confused Ram. They both should have known, should have seen what HarThass was about. The Seer had ways of secrecy that were terrifying. Ram knew that to be tired decreased his powers, and that angered him too. There were such subtle skills yet to learn, ways to avoid his weaknesses—but how could he learn them here, when his job was to keep them safe on the mountain?

The clouds hung low and heavy. There had been rain farther down, their clothes were wet and cold. Resolutely they moved on, following the narrow precipitous trail along the cliff until, late in the afternoon, the trail ended suddenly and sharply. Only a steep drop lay ahead. The cliff wall on their right, which continued upward a long way, was sheer, broken only by wrinkles of stone inches wide, far too narrow for even an agile goat to climb. Ram swallowed. "We can't go back! There isn't time to go back, the Seer's army will sweep into Burgdeeth, Jerthon—Jerthon will need the help of the Runestone. I must—I must hold that power against the Seer. . . ."

Fawdref stood leaning over the lip of the trail, staring down into the valley. Cautiously the children looked, and there across the far green valley floor an immense snakelike shadow writhed. "Gantroed," Ram breathed. The shadow oozed closer to the cliff wall directly beneath them, then disappeared into the shadow of the cliff itself.

Skeelie whispered, "Can it climb the cliff?"

"Of course it can. You know what it's like, those legs—they can grip anything."

Fawdref turned his steady gaze on Ram, then looked upward. He spoke in Ram's mind with an intention that chilled Ram; Ram touched the pale, soft fur along the wolf's muzzle, then laid his head against the great rounded skull, swept by the power of Fawdref's thoughts—swept by terror at what Fawdref meant to do.

"You could do it alone, but you can't. . . ." He stared at Fawdref. "You can't balance with *our* weight. It's too sheer, a goat couldn't. . . ."

Fawdref let him know that he could.

Reluctantly Ram shed his pack. He felt weak and uncertain. They could die here—and they must not die. He slipped the last of the mountain meat into his tunic, then began to remove his sword belt; but Fawdref nosed it back. They could hear a crunching sound from the cliff below, heard some rocks break away. Ram dared not look down at the valley again. He glanced at Skeelie and knew she felt the same. He felt Fawdref's strength reach to steady him. He was weak with terror. He would rather fight the gantroed, he would . . . Fawdref nosed at him again. He looked into Fawdref's eyes, then at last he climbed obediently onto the great wolf's back, all power within him silent now, withheld in mortal fear; he was a tiny child again, wanting comforting.

He turned to look at Skeelie. She was so deathly white he thought she could not do it.

Skeelie shed her pack and lay herself atop Rhymannie's back, her legs bent and gripping, her arms tight around the bitch wolf's neck, her face in Rhymannie's thick coat. Her eyes were closed tight.

Ram felt the lump of the wolf bell wedged between his ribs and Fawdref's back and forgot helplessness then, beginning to pour all the skills he knew into the bell's power—the bell was not a vessel to command wolves now, but a source of strength for them all.

HARTHASS DISMOUNTED. A soldier took his reins and led his horse onto the scow. The wind was still, the narrow inlet clear and calm. On the other side, Farr looked small and ragged. Both scows smelled so strongly of fish it was no wonder the horses balked. It had taken the fool Farrians half the morning to get their catch unloaded and the scows ready for passage. He boarded the larger scow and stood at the rail.

The water was the color of dead grass, but clear enough; he could see the dark shapes of the sunken islands deep down, and the outline of Opensa's sunken towers. He caught a sense of alarm suddenly from the young Seer, AcShish, and reached out to see why the swarthy boy stood staring so intensely toward the mountains.

HarThass let the vision fill his mind; then slowly he began to smile. He saw the wolves crouching, preparing to scale the sheer cliff, the children clinging. He saw the gantroed hidden below them, seeking, sliding up the sheer wall, led and nurtured by the aura of dark that he, Har-Thass, had so skillfully woven around the children, taught his apprentices to hold. The aura moved with them constantly up the mountains, bringing the gantroed now, out from its slimy stone den into daylight it may not have touched for centuries. He raised his hand—he could flick wolves and children from that wall in one quick surge of power, into the gantroed's jaws.

Yet, did he want to kill Ramad so soon? Might he not, even yet, seduce the boy into turning back? Or, better, seduce him into bringing the Runestone down the mountain to him? A moment of uncertainty gripped him. He stared blindly up toward Tala-charen, seeing the wolves crouched.

And then quickly he sent his powers in a dark sudden surge. The gantroed writhed more agilely up that rock wall toward the children. He would turn them back, delay them, weaken them further. . . . Let them live yet awhile.

But he met a jolt of violence, sickening him: his own force was gripped and twisted back. He stared into the element of dark and saw Jerthon facing him, laughing. *Laughing!* He trembled with fury; he would see Jerthon burn. He felt his five apprentices drawn taut against Jerthon, and still their power, all together, was not sufficient. Those slaves! Those damnable, fracking slaves. And they stood as one with the wolves and with that impossible boy and his bell, grown stronger, grown beyond tolerating.

JERTHON FORGOT the pot of molten bronze in his hands as he knelt before the forge fire, his mind, his very soul on the dark peaks, caught in battle as he stood with Ram to drive HarThass back, to slow the gantroed as the great wolf crouched to leap. He pulled the silence of death from the far world of night and flung it down on Har-Thass, pulled the force of earth from the mountains themselves, from the morass of stone and sent it down on the Pellian to snarl his web of terror and the insidious illusion of uncertainty he spun. And Fawdref tensed.

Ram, his face against the great wolf's shaggy neck, could see the sky out beyond the cliff, the peaks far below, see dark clouds rolling closer. He felt Fawdref measure the spans, one above the next, gauge where each foot would strike and cling. Once Fawdref made that first surging leap there could be no stopping or his weight and Ram's would pull them back to spill them into the valley. His first momentum must keep them moving upward in one terrible, straining effort until they stood at last safe on the crest—or until they failed, and fell.

The wolf sprang suddenly upward in a rending surge of raw power that took Ram's breath, an explosion from crouching haunches that lifted them high up the cliff, clinging, paws scrabbling, leaped again, straining up and up the mountain, leaning into the cliff's side. Again upward. . . .

Rhymannie mimicked him, came flying up. Each leap Fawdref made, she made also as Skeelie clung in empty terror.

Five leaps, six. Ram expected to feel the momentum reverse and know they would plunge down. He willed Fawdref upward, made himself as a feather on Fawdref's back, weightless. . . .

And at last Fawdref stood on the crest of solid rock. Ram loosed his arms from the shaggy neck, felt his feet strike the ground. He turned to look at Skeelie. She slipped down off Rhymannie's back and grinned at him.

They were on a thin, long ridge that ran through space to join a mountain and fell away on both sides to the valleys below. Mountain peaks lay below them like a carpet, fading into the far horizons. And beyond the first mountain they faced, rose a second: taller and very thin; symmetrical as a tower. Tala-charen. There was no mistaking it. It thrust above the mountain ranges and into the sky like a castle meant to rule clouds, meant to be approached only on the winds. And those winds bit at them with icy fingers as they began to cross along the crest of the ridge.

But the ground was warm, and ahead of them steam rose through cracks in the stone, and there was a red glow over the cracked ground and tongues of flame licked out. The other wolves had scaled the cliff and now began to slip past Fawdref light-footed, to go on up the ridge toward the first peak as if they wanted quickly away from the burning stone.

THE SCOWS PULLED into Farr's shore, HarThass swearing roundly at the ineptness of apprentice Seers who were no more help to him than a clutch of hens. To let the gantroed go sluggish as a garden worm, unable to climb to the ledge in time to turn the children back. When his horse was brought, he snatched at the reins with such violence that the animal reared and plunged away and had to be caught again, sending soldiers and apprentices alike into a flurry of confusion. He mounted, jerking the creature's mouth so it nearly unseated him. The apprentices—seething at his anger and at their own failure at such a simple thing and shamed by their master's failure—smirked at his discomfort and looked the other way.

They rode up through Farr's southern village scowling at the staring populace until all but the bravest stepped back inside their doors out of sight. HarThass's angry mood did not abate until they were well on up the river Owdneet and nearly into Aybil. This was low, marshy country. The soldiers killed some ducks for supper and a large water snake. They would eat, rest for two hours, and move on as soon as the moons gave them light.

TAYBA KNEW RAM was in danger. She yearned to reach out to him, was frozen with fear for him and could do nothing. She did not know what danger, only that dark powers swung and tilted around him, tried to force her to stand with them against him; to give herself to them. But she had nothing to give, would never stand against Ram, was unable to deal with this. She felt herself torn, knelt weeping and did not know why she wept; felt gentleness touch her, seduce her, felt the darkness soothe and warm her, drug her. . . .

WHERE THE RIDGE joined the first peak, a cave led into the mountain. The children, pressing close to the wolves, entered the cave gladly after so much height and empty space around them, sighed with relief at the closeness of stone walls. Even the dim light seemed pleasant, and the protection very welcome, for it had started to rain again and that high ridge had been terrifying in the sweeping rain.

They drew deeper into the cave, and deeper. The dim light took on a red glow, dull red pulsing along the cave walls. After several turnings they came to a lake of fire, red molten rock bubbling, sending out a heat that at first was lovely, then as they drew closer made them hesitate, was so hot they wanted to turn away from it. A narrow ledge ran beside the burning lake, against the sheer wall. Beyond the lake the cave widened. They saw dark shadows move there, then disappear. "We—we had best go on," Ram said.

"But the shadows. . . ."

He started across, his jaw clenched. It would be worse

if they stayed. "The gantroed is still behind us somewhere," he said quietly.

TAYBA FELT THE DARK soothe her, caress and join with her; and gently she gave herself to it. As the children and their companions started along the path beside the burning lake, she knew only the seduction of that unknown warmth and yielded to it, let it wrest a power from her she did not know she gave, felt herself lifted and reaching out with some greater strength than her own.

Jerthon, alarmed, came into her mind quickly and directly, made her see him, stared into her eyes so her own eyes widened. Made her see Ram then, see what she was about: and the power within her exploded outward in a violent wrenching that sent a wolf sprawling toward the burning lake; she screamed, terrified, drew back, pulled back, twisting away from the dark. Saw Jerthon's mind and heart reach out to catch the burned wolf and lift her to safety.

She knelt breathless and sick. What had happened? She did not want to see, to face it. She pushed Jerthon away in panic; and he turned from her willingly, sick at what she had done, allowed to be done. HarThass had shaped a skill over her that appalled him.

Ram saw, in that instant when he and Skeelie together snatched at the falling wolf and felt Jerthon's power with them—in that instant he knew Tayba's confusion and her betrayal. He went sick at the knowledge. Not only his life and the wolves, but so much more—she jeopardized it all. He could not bear to think she would, yet it was so. She had let the dark power in, had welcomed it simply by denying her own power. And now—now, for the rest of the journey up into Tala-charen, she was likely to betray them again. *Tayba—Mamen.* . . . He was faint with the heat of the burning lake that boiled beside their hurrying feet, was dizzy with the hot, steaming air. His anger at Tayba seemed one with the heat, he was light-headed, dizzy and sick. . . .

IT WAS GROWING increasingly difficult for the slaves to hide their plans from HarThass as the Seer drew closer to Burgdeeth—if, indeed, he did not already know of the

150

Burgdeeth—if, indeed, he did not already know of the tunnel and the importance they placed on it. A tunnel to lie like a talisman of freedom beneath Burgdeeth. A hidden place, a place of safety for generations yet unborn. If they failed to take the town, and Venniver's religion became a reality, it would be there always to harbor those who would escape. And if they took the town, the tunnel would become a bulwark against attack, where women and children could hide from the cruelty and maiming that a later Herebian attack could bring. A tunnel from which the vibrations of the relics of the past and the vibrations of the statue would speak out to young Seers.

HarThass would destroy it if he knew; and HarThass was far too capable of digging deep down into one's mind, to seek out just such knowledge.

"YOU SEE!" EnDwyl said. "Even with all that, she botched it. She's too unpredictable. She—"

"Those cursed apprentices botched it!" HarThass scowled at the five rigid backs riding ahead of them, then looked at EnDwyl piercingly. He did not admit his own failure. "Given a little more time, I'll have the girl as carefully fettered as this stupid animal I ride. Meantime, they are not past the burning lake yet—wait and see what my" —he raised his voice threateningly—"what my skilled apprentices will do to them before they are past it." He kicked his mount brutally and sent it up into the bit to bow its neck in useless effort in HarThass's idea of spirit.

EnDwyl gave him a sideways glance, then looked away across the low hills that flanked the plain. The horses were growing tired, they didn't need HarThass's stupid treatment. He stared at the plain, the hills, and thought that if they—*when* they took Burgdeeth, they would take all this land as well. His thoughts were broken suddenly as HarThass jerked his horse to a clumsy halt and sat like a dead weight in the saddle. EnDwyl reined in beside him. The other five Seers had reined up too, turned, looking disconcerted. The soldiers turned in their saddles to eye them with patient annoyance.

HarThass, still as stone, began to sweat with the force he was using in some cold effort; at last he said, raising

151

his eyes to the other Seers, "You fracking incompetents! Even without the girl to hinder you, you can't—I did not mean for them all to get by that molten lake! Not *all*. What were you about? Daydreaming. You could have put a wolf or two in to boil!" He glared at EnDwyl as if it were his fault too and kicked the gray in the ribs to vent his anger, went lurching off at a gallop that nearly unseated him as the animal shied around a boulder.

He was no great horseman, the Seer of Pelli.

RAM AND SKEELIE stood some yards beyond the boiling lake, the wolves clustered around them. The wolf who had nearly fallen in lay licking her burned leg. They had barely made it across as the Seer of Pelli sent a second sickening force to topple and unnerve them; had clung creeping along the damp wall, the heat nearly unbearable, singeing whiskers and faces, the Seer's force pulling them like a magnet toward that boiling mass; had tumbled at last onto cool, firm stone nearly breathless.

Skeelie said, "Well at least our clothes are dry. We *were* cold, we wanted to be warm."

"Warm. Not singed." He knelt to examine Celic's burned leg. They didn't even have water to ease the burn —and all of them were thirsty now—no salve to help her, nothing. They stared back at the flaming lake, then turned away from it, sick at the close escape. The smell of burning flesh and hair filled the cave.

Red reflections from the fiery lake glanced across the cave walls. The hurt bitch moaned, then was still. She was a gentle, deep gray little wolf. "Celic," Ram said. "Celic." She looked at him with kindness in spite of the pain. They went on at last, Celic hopping on three feet. The cave grew smaller, then larger again, always lit by a dull light as if fissures opened somewhere above them. When they made a crude camp at last, the wolves paced guard, several at a time, as the children slept. They came, near to noon the next day, to a honeycombed expanse through which they must crawl. Blind white lizards scuttled away, stirred by their vibrations against the stone. Skeelie shivered. "We must be near the other side of the mountain by this time. And we keep dropping."

"That will make the climb longer, up into Tala-charen."

"There's nothing growing, no morliespongs, our food won't last long if. . . . ."

"Maybe—maybe between the mountains something will be growing. We'll need water. There's nothing, just those trickles in the rock." The children had lapped at the damp rock just as the wolves had, absorbing every drop into their dry throats.

The cave grew narrower, the ceiling lower. They were so thirsty. The weight of the mountain above them was oppressive. Celic kept up on her three legs very well. Ram felt the powers converging on Burgdeeth, knew that the slaves would come out soon through the completed statue, to challenge Venniver. That the Pellians were drawing close to Burgdeeth. The power that lay in Tala-charen could help Jerthon; and without it, the battle would be bloody indeed, very close. He pressed on, pale and silent.

The tunnel grew very tight, almost completely dark. HarThass's darkness rode with them; the mountain whispered with voices that touched their minds then vanished. "I'm afraid," Skeelie said quietly, but did not slack her pace. Something cold pushed past them unseen; the air stirred suddenly.

Then in the distance they saw flame blocking the tunnel, a nearly human figure with fire playing over its warty hide. Ram felt out to touch its sullen cruelty; then slowly and carefully he spun a web of confusion, deluding, misleading until at last it turned away into some dark fissure. When they passed the narrow opening, they saw its red reflection moving. Fire ogre. "Cruel, but mindless," Ram said to reassure himself; but it didn't reassure him.

And he felt the gantroed, knew it crawled in caves directly above them, ever pacing them.

"There's a stair ahead," Skeelie said. "Look." They could just make out a narrow, twisting stair leading upward; they ran, began to climb at once, feeling their way with care, clinging to the stone steps. The wolves growled at something Ram could not sense and pushed on quickly upward.

Finally they thought the air was fresher; then they began to see the steps clearly, and there was light coming down from above them. Soon they could see the stormy sky and feel the damp wind in their faces. They came up out of the well of stairs into the sky; and ahead rose Tala-charen, its peak lost in cloud. They had only to cross the green saddle of valley that ran like a bridge across empty sky. The setting sun cast one harsh orange streak beneath the boiling clouds, then disappeared.

They started down across the meadow, and when their feet touched soft grass, the wolves lapped moisture from the blades. Ram turned to wait for them and felt the mountain lurch, the earth beneath them jolt sickeningly. He grabbed Skeelie, threw her down as the wolves went belly low. The mountain rocked. Ram felt the Seer's power, knew HarThass would wait no longer. The ground rocked so hard he thought the earth would tear away. The empty spaces below them heaved up. "Crawl!" he shouted uselessly, for they were all crawling across the swaying meadow. "Get into Tala-charen."

They could see its entrance, a thin opening, dark. And then suddenly fire ogres appeared in that dark hole, blinking as if the tumult of the earth had driven them from sleep. Ram tried to stand up, feet apart, and the valley shook, and the lower peaks tipped and swam. Thunder echoed. Fawdref pushed close to him. They were spun toppling again, clinging to the unstable earth.

The entrance to Tala-charen blurred, was lost in a burst of flame as more fire ogres emerged. The wolves moved forward, teeth bared. All the forces of Ere seemed to converge as the two mountains lurched. Stones broke away, went tumbling down. They heard a crack and saw flame burst from a peak far below.

At last they had crossed the rocking valley, knelt against the mountain in terror as boulders rolled and fell crashing. The fire ogres came toward them, ranked close, reaching. Skeelie's knife was poised to strike; she screamed without sound. Fawdref leaped, and the stink of burning fur filled the wind. Ram grabbed him, wrapped his arms around him to extinguish flame, shouting the words of the bell: demanding. An ogre had Celic, flame

154

covered her. Wolves cried out as they bit through flame. "Now!" Ram screamed, his fury more than his own; and caught his breath as rain came crashing, thundering down at his bidding.

The flames were drowned. Naked fire ogres like great toads fled falling over stones, back into the fissure. The wolves rolled in rain, killing fire. Ram stroked and stroked their poor burned faces.

They ran at last through the entrance, drenched, safe as long as they remained wet; ran past flame-filled caves, past staring eyes, fiery hands reaching then drawn back, to a spiral flight thin as glass; ran, loving the clammy feel of their wetness as they surged upward, wolves and children; and heard the ogres start up the steps behind them.

Chapter Eleven

VENNIVER REACHED to spear some roast stag from the tray Tayba held, then returned to his argument with Theel. He hardly noticed her. ". . . doesn't matter, he's of no use now, I'm finished with him. The statue . . ."

"He could be of use," Theel said dryly. "Making tools. The forgeman—there's a lot needed. One forgeman can't—"

"We'll have more craftsmen soon. Next time we go down into Zandour to trade."

"I suppose so," Theel said. "The Seer *is* a trouble-maker."

She turned away, sick at what Venniver intended; sick with the unease that had gripped her all afternoon, that held her now with such power that every movement seemed an effort. Her mind was hazy, confused. She heard Venniver say, "He could make problems. We. . . ." Her thoughts turned coldly to the statue in the square.

She had stood beneath gathering storm clouds just before she came in to serve supper, led inexorably to the square to stare up at the complete statue, the rearing bronze god, the winged horses lifting against a last harsh slash of sun that died quickly. She had been touched with awe at its beauty, but had felt something else, too. Something imminent and secret and upsetting. The statue was completed. Something would happen now. *Was* happening. Ram's danger was part of it—and a seething, terrible turmoil in the minds around her that she could not—would not—decipher. That was part of it. Forces looming, drawing in . . . the statue. . . .

But her mind led her away from the statue in a morass of confusion, away from some knowledge. She could not settle, stood staring at the roast stag, the smell of its nauseating her. What force was all around her, pressing at her? She closed her eyes. What was it she should know? The statue—she felt Jerthon push into her mind suddenly, taking away that which she had almost seen, almost known. She stood scowling, her hands like ice.

Confused and frustrated, she left the dining hall at last to stand in the door to the street.

The damp rising wind changed direction, fitful as a cat. The clouds lay low, heavy as stone. Rain would come soon. The fading light was gray and dull. As she turned, she saw a figure slipping behind a building; a slave, she thought, a slave alone and free, hiding in shadow. Yes, the slave called Pol. Thin, freckled beneath a thatch of red hair. Hiding from the guards. Why was he . . . ? And suddenly and clearly, a vision flooded her mind. She stood hardly breathing; Seeing, knowing; knew the slaves had escaped; knew Jerthon's plan, every detail in one terrifying instant.

They had come out of the statue's hollow base through a little door. Even now while she stood staring at the empty street, they were moving through the town unseen, attacking the guards in the tower, taking the weapons there, breaking the cell door from without to make it seem that was their way of escape; were sealing the hole in the cell floor with mortar, sealing the side tunnel into the pit. They had left only a little hole up into the grove among boulders; that, and the entrance in the statue, its door so cleverly made that a man could stare right at it and never know it was there.

She knew where more weapons were cached. She knew where Dlos had hidden food in the storeroom. She turned, drawing in her breath. At that moment slaves were slipping down the corridors of the Hall behind her, stealing into rooms, snatching up weapons. She clutched at the wall, fear gripping her, and a terrible urgency.

They meant to take Burgdeeth. Her pulse was pounding. Venniver would die this night. She felt a terrible tenderness for him suddenly, a oneness with him that she had never felt for another—in spite of his cruelty. Because of his cruelty, perhaps. Because of his genius. Burgdeeth as he planned it would die this night. The Temple, the beautiful Set . . . Venniver's dream.

She fled back into the hall. Venniver was laughing at some joke; she could not make him listen, shook his shoulder impatiently, driven by urgency; and sickened by something that tried to silence her. Venniver turned, scowling, as she fought for breath.

"What is it? What?"

"The slaves, they. . . ." The battle within her was fierce, as if hands gripped her and twisted her away. She could hardly speak. "The slaves," she choked at last, "the slaves are out—with weapons."

The guards were on their feet, snatching up swords and sectbows, Theel staring at her for a moment then hurrying away. Venniver held her wrist in a steel grip. "How? How did they get out?"

"I don't know. I saw them in the street. I don't know how, they—*they will kill you!*" She felt sick at what she was doing, could not control her trembling.

He loosed her wrist, rose, and swung away from her. She stood staring after him in turmoil; and she saw Ram suddenly in a vision against the boiling sky as if he stood on top of the world, saw him thrown to the ground, falling, boulders pelting down, and felt immense forces battling there. Then she saw riders pounding fast up along the river toward Burgdeeth, their horses slick with rain, their wet capes whipping in the wind, their faces—*EnDwyl*. EnDwyl and the Pellian Seers approaching fast as Venniver's guards battled slaves in the dark streets. She was Seeing, she thought, swallowing. Seeing—*willing herself to See*.

She saw Jerthon's eyes then, demanding something of her, saw the danger she had wrought for him, his anger; didn't know who was right or if there was a right. She saw men locked in battle, men fall in their own blood; she stood gripping the edge of the table, her knuckles white.

The slaves would die because of her. Would die. *Jerthon would die. . . .*

But the dark pulled at her and soothed her. She saw HarThass's soldiers plunge across the river into the streets, saw Jerthon facing two guards in desperate battle. She heard Ram scream out in fury, fierce as death itself.

She ran out into the street, stood staring in panic at the bloody fighting, saw a slave lying dead beside the steps.

She knelt, opened the dead man's fingers, and slipped his bloody sword from his hand.

THE CHILDREN RAN UP the spiraling flight past rooms open to the winds, and heard fire ogres screaming behind them; past bright rooms and saw only flashing colors as they ran, their breaths catching. The flight ended in a fall of water. They dove in, stood beneath the downpour as the red flame of fire ogres drew close outside, gibbering, unable to enter.

They came out soaking into a beautiful room, its window thick in the mountain wall, its curved benches deep with bright pillows. At one side a flight led up. They climbed. No one had breath to speak. In the next chamber, water fell again, and in the next. Twelve chambers led upward, and outside the windows the sky darkened, and rain came whipping to damp the thick sills. Lightning broke the night, and thunder; and that other dark rose with them, an incubus they could not shake. And as the wolves gazed upward, the lust of killing came into their eyes. Ram stopped on a stair and took Fawdref's heavy head in his hands. The great wolf's eyes were full of a need that chilled and excited him; and Fawdref's mind gave back only silence.

"They want to kill," Skeelie breathed, watching. She stared upward toward the unseen hollow peak of Tala-charen. "What is up there? They. . . ."

"Whatever it is, HarThass—HarThass is there too. His forces are in Burgdeeth, are fighting Jerthon, bloody in the streets, in the dark rain." He swallowed. "But he is there above us too—waiting."

They hurried on, the wolves predatory and stalking. They came at last to the top of Tala-charen, into a cave lit softly by the glowing stone of the floor, as if they stood on a lake of bright water. Skeelie stared at it, hesitating to step, as if it would give way. "What is it?"

159

"Termagant. You know, in the myth of the sea god, the stone that catches daylight and holds it for the night."

She stared, then stepped delicately. And as their eyes grew accustomed, the cave seemed to brighten even more. The walls undulated around the curved open space in the natural formation of the mountain, with a ceiling curving down, a smooth dome decorated all over with inlaid stone in the patterns of animals: the triebuck, mythical creatures, and stag and winged horses and birds, great golden lizards, flying snakes colored like jewels.

It was quite empty, a cool empty room; yet the wolves stood growling, heads lowered. And as the children watched, they became increasingly uneasy. A mist began to form. Only a darkness at first in the center of the cave. Then a deep shadow. Then a cloud, thick and growing heavy.

And it was more than a cloud: it was a shape growing thicker until soon its writhing mass filled the cave. Snake-like, coiling, pushing against walls and ceiling.

Its blunt head sought them, its tongue licked out, its tendrils reached to caress them. Its hungry mouth was fanged, its breath stinking of death. Its pale eyes watched them, and it knew why they had come.

TAYBA WIPED BLOOD from the sword where the slave's hand had held it, hefted it to get the feel of the grip, then slipped out into the street.

Men shouted, she could hear swords clash; rain swept in her face, dark shapes lurched, appeared suddenly in the downpour and disappeared. She dodged lunging men to search, nearly fell over a fallen, screaming horse. Her hands shook, she ran with fear crowding her—and the dark leading her; knew Venniver and Jerthon had met in battle, ran—there, in the alley.

The dark pulled her on. She felt horror, suddenly and sharply, and did not know why. She reached the alley, saw Venniver's sword flash through rain. She gripped cold metal. Fury and eagerness took her. She stared at Jerthon. . . .

Then suddenly she went dizzy, was ignobly sick against the stone wall.

160

Afterward she crouched, drenched and shivering, very ill, staring at the battle; not knowing what she had wanted to do or why she had come. Metal rang as a sword struck stone. "Venniver," she whispered, her lips numb.

THE GANTROED'S TENDRILS snaked out; its open mouth wanted blood. Ram dared not take his eyes from it, felt HarThass in it. Fawdref leaped again, the wolves tore at it. Ram hacked snaking tendrils from the great worm, then he raised the bell. His own power seemed small. The beast twisted, a tendril seared his arm. Tendrils flashed around Fawdref, choking him. The wolf fought, snarling, fangs cutting deep. The gantroed coiled tighter. Ram screamed the words of the bell, reached to tear power from Ere's night; and the gantroed had Skeelie, pulling her flailing toward its hairy mouth. She knifed at the great tongue; the creature screamed and loosed her.

Ram saw Jerthon fall in battle, saw Tayba. . . .

Wolves were knocked away by flailing tendrils, leaped again. The gantroed reared, Ram plunged his sword into its pale stomach. It coiled over them screaming. Ram went sick at Tayba's intent. A wolf leaped, knocked him away as the gantroed struck, its teeth grazing him. He brought his sword across it, into the worm, but his mind was filled with Tayba, his power was with Tayba, turning her, forcing her. Wolves clung like flies to the stinking hide. The coils grew smaller, crushing them. The creature's blood flowed yellow. Ram felt the dark forces sway; then he saw with surprise that Skeelie was far back in the cave, nearly crushed by the swinging coils.

She crouched beneath the gantroed, dodging as she searched along the cave walls. The snake slammed against her, slapped at her mindlessly with its wormlike arms as it fought Ram and the wolves. Ram rolled away from the churning wolves and ran. Behind him wolves leaped in unison for the gantroed's head. He heard Skeelie scream, thought she was crushed; he slipped, fell, was pressed into a corner as tentacles lashed him—but he felt the power drumming, a different power now.

He rose, fought to reach her, saw her tearful, frantic

face as she searched wildly along the wall with clutching hands. "I can—there is something. I can feel it, but it won't come clear for me. Ram. . . ."

He touched the wall, and it vibrated under his fingers. He felt along it, his fingers sensitive. The gantroed lunged into them, knocking them against the wall. Something— *there*. The power came strong. He drew out his knife and began to dig at the stone, a bull's heavy form—yes. Behind it an empty space. He pried stones out, they fell away to lie scattered across the floor.

Inside lay the cask, carved of pale wood.

Ram drew it out, held it with shaking hands, oblivious to the battle, to everything. Felt the spell on it, saw his fingers try to lift the lid, watched his hands pry at it uselessly.

The dark reached, needed to blind him. He could feel HarThass close. He brought his forces trembling against the Seer; saw Tayba's sword raised. . . .

He shouted into the screaming storm. Wind lashed through the chamber.

TAYBA FACED Jerthon quietly, then looked down at Venniver, fallen and bleeding, looked with shock at her blood-covered blade. Jerthon said softly, "You meant to kill me. Why did you change your mind?"

"I could—I could do nothing else." She stared and stared at Venniver, could feel his pain. Was he dying? Had she killed him? Then she looked up at Jerthon and knew she truly could have done nothing, *nothing* else but save this tall, fierce man who stood before her drenched with rain and blood, searching her face with an honesty he had, at last, forced her to accept.

They saw too late the soldiers leaping through rain to block the alley, dark shapes in darkness, lurching forward; saw HarThass, cape blowing, sword drawn.

Tayba and Jerthon stood together to face the challenge as, behind them, Venniver rolled onto his side and tried to rise; and suddenly all was confusion, and time twisted with a jolting shock and held cold. Space and time were asunder. The alley and cave were as one. Soldiers poised; Ram's fingers reached to touch the stone; the mountain rocked. Lightning flashed in a jagged bolt that turned the cave pale, made the gantroed look white. The lightning seared Ram's hand, struck the Runestone.

It shattered.

The stone lay white hot in his hands. Nine long shards of jade, glowing white.

Then they began to cool. Turned pale green, then darker until they were the deep color of the sea. The Runestone of Eresu, broken apart. The power shattered. Ram stared at the stones, shocked. Felt their terrible weight. Felt the power that remained; it was the same power, only divided. Not whole, not. . . .

The mountain trembled again, and the floor beneath their feet began to crack, a long, jagged wound growing wider. They leaped back as the dark abyss widened. The dying gantroed began to slip down into the emptiness.

In Burgdeeth, Venniver rose slowly and painfully to his feet. Jerthon held him captive and held the soldiers back with his threat to Venniver. They watched silently as HarThass approached.

Ram reached to give Jerthon power from the stone he held. And in the cave hazy figures had suddenly appeared all around him, ghostly figures growing clearer. A girl with long brown hair leaped from the back of a winged horse to run toward them; a red-haired young man turned to stare at Ram; a man dressed in blue robes looked up in surprise; others, a pale, lovely young woman who gazed into Ram's eyes with such recognition that he went giddy with a feeling he had never encountered.

The figures stood with hands cupped upward in ceremony. Ram's hands were the same, palms up. And the terrible weight of the jade shards was lighter; for now only one section of the Runestone lay in his palm. He stood staring at it, stricken with the shattering of the stone, the shattering of that perfect power. Felt the power of the one stone, though. Saw that in those other, ghostly hands, lay shards of jade. Two? Three? He could not be sure. But there had been nine.

Had some gone, then, careening down into the dark abyss? As he stared down into the emptiness, the jagged cavern began to narrow, to close. They all drew back, watching; the ghostly crew mingling quite comfortably among wolves.

The floor closed slowly until only a jagged black scar marred the cave floor. This remained. The gantroed's bones, white and clean, protruded from it; wedged deep in the mountain, perhaps to mingle with the lost jade.

JERTHON HELD the soldiers frozen, felt HarThass's power like a tide. He glanced at Tayba. "Are you with me? Help me hold them." She felt him draw her out. She swallowed, brought her power stronger to lift and surge upward, catching her breath. How did she know to do this? Jerthon faced HarThass, swords clashed; their figures spun, were as one in the dark alley; she held the soldiers back, held Venniver back, straining; gasped as HarThass went down and Jerthon stood over him, his sword at the Pellian's throat; turned away with shock at the Seer's quick death.

But they could not hold Venniver long. He rose, came at them bleeding. She faced him sword drawn, as Jerthon whirled and had him in a grip like steel. She stared into Venniver's eyes, could not speak, his hatred chilling her through. Would Jerthon kill him?

But Jerthon backed away from the guards, Venniver his captive. "He can't hold that rabble forever."

"Even—even with the power of the stone? Ram—"

"Even with Ram's power, in that one shard of jade. HarThass's apprentices are well trained—out there somewhere. Can't you feel them?" He glanced at Venniver, held tight against him, then at her, appraising her. "This one will buy our freedom. If it is freedom you want." He was watching her, but she could only look at Venniver. His hatred was terrible, she stared back at him, sick. Yet that hard, confining shell around herself had cracked away. Something new was determined to live, something beyond what she had known with Venniver. Something more real and urgent than anything in her life. She looked at Venniver and swallowed, looked away. Her tears were mixed with rain, salt and bitter.

She stood beside Jerthon and, in a power she had never admitted, never wanted, she held with him, held the sol-

164

diers back. A power that rose, now, from the very core of her being. She stayed the guards, the Pellian Seers, her mind coolly linked with Jerthon's. They forced Venniver down the street toward the band of mounts that waited, guarded by Dlos. Some of the horses were saddled, some roped together. Derin and Saffoni led horses forward. Tayba could not speak for the effort she made to hold strong against the Pellian forces, against Venniver's stifled guards. How long she could hold, she did not know.

Slaves were coming out of the dark, some leading the soldier's horses. The rain had slacked, nearly ceased. She saw men carrying wounded, felt out with Jerthon in quick assessment. He said, "Drudd? Pol?"

"Yes. We are here," Drudd said, lifting a wounded man up. "Trane is dead. And Vanaw. I don't think . . . where are the women?"

Derin rode up, leading saddled horses. "They . . . Barban and Hallel are dead." Her voice caught. "Cirell is here, with Dlos. We . . . must we leave our dead?"

"Yes," Jerthon said shortly. The rain had ceased. The clouds began to part so that a little light touched the hurrying band as they mounted and sorted themselves out. Tayba could feel Jerthon's effort with her own, holding their pursuers.

Were there still horses there in the dark street that could be used to pursue them? More slaves were coming. But they were not slaves, she thought suddenly. They were free now. At last, all accounted for, they rode quickly out of Burgdeeth, Venniver tied to his mount, furious and silent, his bleeding staunched with rags.

They turned him loose somewhere above Burgdeeth, to struggle home on foot as best he could. Then they loosed their waning hold on the soldiers and guards and heard them shouting back in the town for horses they would never find.

RAM AND SKEELIE lay on their stomachs in the deep window of the room where they had slept, staring down the steep side of Tala-charen at the wild, empty land. Ram said, "We'll go down this way, come out in that long valley."

"But we came the other way, into the other side of the mountain. How—"

"I think . . . I just feel that we can. We'll have to see. Those stairs—didn't you wonder how Tala-charen could crack apart but leave the rooms untouched? Didn't you—"

"Oh, I figured that out," she said offhandedly. "There, where the mountain bows out. The crack is in there, the other side of the caves." She stared at Ram, giving him a picture.

She had waked at first light to climb up onto this sill and lie so, looking out at the sun-touched peaks of the lower mountains to the northwest, Tala-charen's shadow cast long across them. She had seen where the crack in Tala-charen might be. She had slid down from the sill and gone down the spiraled flight to the next room, and the next below it. There the wall was cracked too, the gantroed's bones pushing through. She had reached in among those bones to search with blind fingers; but no shard of jade had she found, had turned away at last, disappointed. Nothing in that dark crack but bones and more bones. She turned to look at Ram.

"Why did the stone shatter? After all that climb and nearly getting killed, the cliff, the fiery lake—if you were meant to have the stone, why did it shatter?"

"It just did," he said simply. "No one planned it. I wasn't *meant* to have the stone—the time was just right that I seek it."

She only stared at him.

"You don't think . . . ? The forces on Ere . . . everything was right for me to seek out the stone, but no one planned that I do it. And no one said, 'Now we will shatter it.' " He watched her, frowning a little. "Mostly it was HarThass's power, though. He waited too long, he played me too long, like a clumsy fisherman. And then when it was too late he threw all his power into the shattering of the stone, to destroy it. And with the other forces there, wheeling, all that power. . . ." He spread his hands. "It—is shattered."

"But those others, those who came and held the stone then. That wasn't accident, Ram!"

166

"Yes it was. It was accident. All—all those forces, balanced like that for an instant, threw—threw us outside of time. And those who desired the power for good—somehow they got through. Maybe—maybe there were others among them. I don't know. Now," he said with awe, "in other times there are shards of jade like this one. Power, Skeelie. All strewn across time. Because of accident, because of a clashing of powers—because of one Seer's lust for power that tipped the scale."

"What—what will happen because of it?"

He stared out over the mountains silently, longing to See all of time spread before him just as the nameless peaks were spread, but seeing only peaks. "No one . . . no one can know, Skeelie."

"How can you be so *sure?* How can you be sure, Ramad of Zandour, that there is not one force making—causing all this to happen?"

"Nobody is *sure,*" he said patiently. "There *is* one force. But it is made of hundreds of forces. You can feel it—a Seer can. But it doesn't make things happen. They just happen. Forces balance, overbalance—that is what makes life; nothing plans it, that would take the very life from all—all the universe.

"But something—something judges," he said with certainty. "In all of it together, there is a judgment."

Fawdref came to push close, and Ram put his arm around the great wolf's neck. "But it is the strength of the force in our little desires for good and evil, Skeelie, that balances and counterbalances and makes things happen. Makes life happen." He stared hard at her. "It is not *planned!* Like—like a recipe for making soap!"

He looked out across the unknown mountains, and she could feel in him the challenge of those forces. He tossled Fawdref roughly, making the great wolf smile. Out there—across the unknown lands and back behind them in the seething, warring countries—there was all of life: to explore, to come to terms with in his new power. What could he do, what good could he help to draw from the balancing, ever-changing forces of Ere? She wanted to be with Ram in this, wherever he went, whatever forces he touched.

He took her hand, and they started down out of Tala-charen toward the north.

They emerged on the other side of the mountain from the place where they had started, stood blinking in the bright sun.

The wolves tasted the air, gave the children a parting nudge, and went to hunt. Ram and Skeelie started up the long valley, wishing they had horses. "I think," Ram said, scanning the mountains on either side, "I think. . . ." He knelt, found a small stone, scraped away grass, and began to draw on the ground. "Here we are in the valley." He drew mountains, another valley, a narrow way around mountains and then a valley beyond that, very wide, dotted by lakes of fire and steaming geysers. And beyond that again, cliffs. Then at last a round valley through which the Owdneet flowed. "They are there; they are beginning to pack up. They will come this way, Jerthon knows we are here. Mamen. . . ." He began to smile. "Mamen knows! Mamen *Sees* us, Skeelie!"

"She—she will be all right."

"Yes. She will."

"Now VENNIVER will go on with his plans for the town," Dlos said, dishing out mawzee cakes, her face flushed from the fire. They had all slept late in the peaceful little valley; the night guards slept still, beyond a pile of pack saddles. She stared at Jerthon. "Is that what you want, Venniver building his little empire?" Her wrinkles deepened in a scowl.

Jerthon gave her a hard, steady look. "It is not what I want, Dlos. Nevertheless, Burgdeeth may prove to be of value."

Dlos stared. "How have you worked that out?"

"Burgdeeth might be," he said shortly, "a place of tempering. A place of testing."

"Testing? You are mad, Jerthon!"

"No, not mad. HarThass is dead. I don't think his apprentices will bother with Burgdeeth. They are—a weak lot. If they had the Runestone, they would. But without it, I think the power of the stone that Ram holds will be enough to stop them." He speared some side meat from the fire, laid it on a slab of bread. "The town is different now. The statue is there. The tunnel is complete, has vibrations of its own. Strong ones. Young Seers born there —if they are of true worth—will have something to lead them, to draw them toward truth. And they will have— a liberal education in what sloth and evil are all about, if they grow up in Venniver's town."

Tayba swallowed her meat with a dry throat. She would not, two days ago, have bothered to speak out, or have cared. "He—he will kill them," she said evenly. "Don't you know he means to kill them, even the babies? To burn them on the altar of the Temple?"

"He means to," Jerthon said. "But that will not come for a while. And before it does, perhaps we will be able to prevent it."

She stared at him and didn't see how anything could prevent Venniver from his plans, as long as he was master of Burgdeeth.

"There are ways," Jerthon said. And would say no more.

THE CHILDREN CAME DOWN a face of rough lava, half sliding, the wolves frolicking across it. Below, horses grazed. The smoke of a campfire rose. A rider spurred her horse out wildly up the hill. Ram began to run.

"Mamen!"

She plunged galloping up through the woods, pulled her horse up and slid from the saddle to hold Ram fast. She was crying, hugged him fiercely. Other riders came galloping. Jerthon rode up quietly and sat looking down at Ram.

Ram took the Runestone from his tunic and handed it to Jerthon.

Jerthon read the runes carven into the one side. Senseless words, for the rest were broken away. "Eternal . . . will sing." He looked at Ram. "Did it sing?"

"If you call thunder a song. It thundered when it broke apart. It exploded in my hand, hot as Urdd!"

Jerthon handed it back.

"But where. . . ." Ram said, watching Jerthon. "We

169

don't know, really, where it's gone. The other parts. The Children out of time. . . ."

"It went into time, and that is all we can know." Jerthon dismounted and laid a hand on Ram's shoulder. "Now, barring something we cannot foresee, in each age from which those Children came, time will warp again, once, in the same way."

"There—there was a girl," Ram said. "A young woman. She—"

"She was out of a future time," Jerthon said.

"You saw her?"

"I saw."

"Well what. . . ." He remembered the pale young woman's look, as if she longed for him. Remembered his own strange feelings.

"Have you ever been in love, Ramad of Zandour?"

"Of course not!" he said indignantly.

"Well, you will be."

When Ram looked up, Fawdref was grinning at him. Rhymannie raised her head in a sly, female look. Ram scowled at Fawdref. "Old dog, what are *you* laughing at?"

But then he grew sad, for Fawdref meant to leave them. "Not yet," he said. "Jerthon goes to Carriol and so do I. You—you could journey with us. At least as far as the grotto."

But Fawdref let him know his band could travel faster alone. That he would see them in the pass behind the great grotto when they reached it, would perhaps bring fresh meat for them. And so the wolves vanished, faded into the wood that flanked the lava flow and were gone as if they had never been; and if Ram had tears, he let no one see.

They made a feast that night of stag and morliespongs and wild tammi, fat otero roasted on the fire. For at dawn they would split forces, some to ride deeper into the unknown lands through which they were passing, to search for new country or to come, at last, back to Carriol with more knowledge of these lands than anyone now had.

Though most would go to Carriol with Jerthon.

"There is much unsettled land in Carriol," he said, leaning back against stones besides the fire, Skeelie snuggled close. "The ancient city of the gods, the town that has grown around it—they are not a country. The time has come when Carriol must become a country or perish. It is not strong enough now to prevent the Herebian on-slaughts that are surely coming."

Ram would follow Jerthon. He would go nowhere else. He stared sleepily into the fire. They would go to Carriol and build a country of freedom and great pleasure.

They slept close beside the campfire, the night sentries keeping watch. Drudd snored, his head propped on his saddle. Derin and dark-haired Saffoni shared a blanket. It seemed strange to Ram to sleep without Fawdref's shaggy warmth. He snuggled close against Tayba, but she was not furry, nor as warm. Ere's two moons hung low in the clear sky; and the star Waytheer rode between them, its power speaking down to the Runestone, and to Ram.

Ram was nearly asleep when he knew Tayba was cry-ing, holding herself rigid, trying not to wake him, shudder-ing as she swallowed her sobs. He turned over, touched her face, felt tears. "Mamen? What is it? What's the mat-ter?"

"I—I don't know what's the matter." She pushed her face against him. "Everything's the matter. I'm afraid."

"But it's all over. You—"

"It's not all over. I'm afraid." She sat up, stared into the dying fire, then turned to look at him. "We would be in Burgdeeth now. Jerthon would have taken it, if it hadn't been for me. I'm scared, Ram. That's all. Just scared of what I am. Go to sleep." She lay down, pulled him close. "Go to sleep. It's all right. I'm done crying."

He could feel little of what tore at her. He guessed it would be all right. They would make it all right between them. He lay staring at the dying fire and now, once awake, could not go back to sleep. Lay thinking of Tala-charen and seeing those other faces, seeing the past and the future come together, hearing the thunder, feeling the heat of the stone in his palm, the mountain rocking. Smell-ing the stink of the gantroed.

He shivered with a terrible fear of what he was born

to; but that passed, and he lay knowing in some depth of himself the strength he would one day hold. He touched the stone, lying warm in his tunic next to the wolf bell, and knew a sharp anticipation of what waited beyond this night; tried again to see forward in time, and again felt only the sharp yearning he could not explain, could simply hold close as he drifted—and then slept.

SHIRLEY ROUSSEAU MURPHY grew up in California riding the horses her father trained. She attended the San Francisco Art Institute and has been a commercial artist and an interior decorator designing everything from breadboxes to beaded wedding gowns. She has written many books for younger readers, and is currently working on the next book in the Children of Ynell Series. Mrs. Murphy lives with her husband in Georgia.

AVON BOOKS PRESENTS
THE BEST IN MYSTERY & SUSPENSE
FOR YOUNG READERS

AVON ◆ CONTEMPORARY READING
FOR YOUNG PEOPLE

☐ Fox Running R. R. Knudson	43760	$1.50
☐ The Cay Theodore Taylor	51037	$1.75
☐ The Owl's Song Janet Campbell Hale	28738	$1.25
☐ The House of Stairs William Sleator	32888	$1.25
☐ Listen for the Fig Tree Sharon Bell Mathis	51854	$1.95
☐ Me and Jim Luke Robbie Branscum	24588	$ .95
☐ None of the Above Rosemary Wells	26526	$1.25
☐ Representing Superdoll Richard Peck	47845	$1.75
☐ Some Things Fierce and Fatal Joan Kahn, ed.	32771	$1.50
☐ The Sound of Chariots Mollie Hunter	26658	$1.25
☐ Guests in the Promised Land Kristin Hunter	27300	$ .95
☐ Taking Sides Norma Klein	41244	$1.50
☐ Sunshine Norma Klein	76307	$2.25
☐ Why Me? The Story of Jennie Patricia Dizenzo	76331	$1.95
☐ Forgotten Beasts of Eld Patricia McKillip	42523	$1.75

Where better paperbacks are sold or directly from the publisher.
Include 50¢ per copy for postage and handling; allow 4-6 weeks for
delivery.

Avon Books, Mail Order Dept.
224 West 57th Street, New York, N.Y. 10019

CRY 7-80

THE BEST IN SCIENCE FICTION
AND FANTASY FROM
AVON ⬡ BOOKS

URSULA K. LE GUIN

The Lathe of Heaven	43547	1.95
The Dispossessed	51284	2.50

ISAAC ASIMOV

Foundation	50963	2.25
Foundation and Empire	42689	1.95
Second Foundation	45351	1.95
The Foundation Trilogy (Large Format)	50856	6.95

ROGER ZELAZNY

Doorways in the Sand	49510	1.75
Creatures of Light and Darkness	35956	1.50
Lord of Light	44834	2.25
The Doors of His Face The Lamps of His Mouth	38182	1.50
The Guns of Avalon	31112	1.50
Nine Princes in Amber	51755	1.95
Sign of the Unicorn	30973	1.50
The Hand of Oberon	51318	1.75
The Courts of Chaos	47175	1.75

Include 50¢ per copy for postage and handling,
allow 4-6 weeks for delivery.

Avon Books, Mail Order Dept.
224 W. 57th St., N.Y., N.Y. 10019